DEAD MAN'S GOLD
A Western Trio

DEAD MAN'S GOLD

A Western Trio

T. T. FLYNN

Five Star • Waterville, Maine

First Edition
First Printing: August 2006

Published in conjunction with Golden West Literary Agency.

Set in 11 pt. Plantin by Carleen Stearns.

Printed in the United States on permanent paper.

Library of Congress Cataloging-in-Publication Data

Flynn, T. T.
    Dead man's gold : a western trio / by T.T. Flynn.—1st ed.
        p. cm.
    ISBN 1-59414-404-4 (hc : alk. paper)
    I. Title.
PS3556.L93A6 2006
    813'.54—dc22   2006003746

DEAD MAN'S GOLD

TABLE OF CONTENTS

Tide of Empire

Argosy began publication as a pulp magazine titled *The Argosy* with the October, 1896 issue. It was published by the Frank A. Munsey Company. In 1917 the magazine became a weekly. While it remained a pulp magazine, *Argosy* changed its trim-size to what is termed bed-sheet with the issue dated January 18, 1941. In 1942 it became a monthly and was sold to Popular Publications. Popular Publications changed the format of the magazine from pulp paper to slick paper with the January, 1943 issue. As a monthly, *Argosy* rarely ran serials, unlike the days when it was a weekly. Rogers Terrill, who as editor of Popular Publications' *Dime Western* and *Star Western* regularly featured stories by T. T. Flynn, contacted Marguerite E. Harper, Flynn's agent, and suggested he write a long story for publication in *Argosy*. "Tide of Empire", as Flynn titled his story, was completed on September 27, 1943. It was accepted at once, but due to considerations of length, it appeared as a three-part serial, beginning with the January, 1944 issue. The title was changed to "Logs for St. Louis" upon publication. The author was paid $900. For its first book appearance the author's title and text have been restored.

I

There were revolver shots down on the freight deck, and a burst of loud voices and rough jeers. But at the card game in the barroom, no one got up to investigate. There were serious matters afoot here, too. Uneasy glances were turned in the direction of Matthew Jordan.

As though in tactful interruption, the great chime whistle of the *Silver Eagle* poured its deep-throated, musical blast upon the early and misty night. In the brightly lighted, extravagantly luxurious barroom the sound was long drawn out, mournful yet nostalgically beautiful as it reached across the Mississippi's current to the Illinois and Iowa banks and returned in whispering echoes.

"I'll meet your thousand, Mister Connally," Matthew Jordan said politely. "And raise you another thousand, sir."

Even the white-aproned bartender looked up from the eggnog he was mixing. He could not have heard the low-voiced words of Matt Jordan. But in that gilt-and-white barroom, colorful with red plush and clustered crystal ceiling lights, attention had heightened visibly in the poker game.

Two elegant gentlemen, known to the bartender as professional riverboat gamblers, walked over and joined the upriver merchants, farmers, rough and prosperous lumbermen, and one buckskin-clad woodsman gathered around the table. The gamblers carried their bourbon glasses with them and stood watching intently.

11

Matt was oblivious to the unusual attention the game was receiving. Big and darkly weathered, he sat as he had for many hours, with an air of musing interest. He had none of the professional's cold and careful mask. His hair, bleached blond by the sun, held hints of reddish gold under the crystal lights; his dark face made the hair seem lighter than it was and emphasized the whiteness of his teeth when he smiled. But the outstanding thing about him was his look of strong self-sufficiency.

Three other men sat at the polished round mahogany table. The gray-bearded lumberman from Prairie du Chien and the wealthy wholesaler from St. Louis had turned in their cards quickly after the deal. They had been doing so for the past half hour, waiting for the stakes to lower.

The fourth player, young Thomas Connally, a mill owner from St. Louis, moved his cards nervously in his long, sensitive fingers, starting slightly as the deep rich blast of the whistle struck again through the night. Connally had been smoking a Cuban cheroot; it had gone dead in his mouth, and he had chewed the end ragged. In his late twenties, a year or two older than Matt Jordan, Connally had a thin, proud face, a carefully polite manner, and an agreeable disposition. The black eyebrows he lifted held direct challenge.

"You interest me, suh. Would another thousand tempt you further?"

Matt chuckled softly. "It would come closer to worrying me. But since my luck seems to be holding, I'll have to be tempted. Would two thousand up please you?"

"And five thousand up!" Connally said without hesitation.

The woodsman, a sturdy fellow whose yellow hair hung neck-length, exclaimed: "Jehosophat! I'd rather face a grizzly than git caught in a game like this."

Connally's laugh was genuine. "My friend," he said, "this is better sport than grizzly hunting. You shoot the bear quickly, suh, or he claws you down, or runs."

"Or I run," amended the woodsman dryly.

The laughter that followed gave relief to the increasing tension. Connally tossed his cigar into the big flare-top brass cuspidor beside the table. His hazel eyes were smoldering with excitement.

"There's no sport in running," he said, smiling. "Jordan, you've turned into a veritable grizzly tonight, suh. No offense meant. You have me looking into the whites of your eyes, suh."

Matt chuckled softly again. "Wish I could be sure you aren't loaded for bear and waiting for the whites of *my* eyes, Connally."

Down on the freight deck loud angry voices, shouts, oaths, whoops of drunken excitement had formed a rough, uneasy background to all other sounds. Now another burst of gunshots was followed by a medley of yells and oaths.

In the barroom men looked at one another. Matt overheard a muttered prophecy: "Sounds like them log raftsmen are gettin' out of hand down there. Ought to be stopped before the lady passengers are frightened."

Matt frowned slightly.

Connally had referred to figures on a slip of paper at his elbow and was writing rapidly on another bit of paper. A faint flush touched his face. He seemed wholly oblivious to the growing tumult on the freight deck below, even when more shots were fired. He looked up, his eyes hot. "It appears that I have lost about twenty-two thousand dollars, suh. You have been kind enough to accept my paper for part of it."

"The stakes have been higher than I wanted," Matt reminded him.

"Sporting of you to allow me, suh," Connally said with a wave of his hand. The dancing excitement deepened in his hazel eyes. "Shortly we'll be at Bank City, where I must go ashore. I have a fine sawmill at Bank City, well worth twice my losses. It will be sporting to play the hand out for the sawmill, suh . . . all or nothing."

Silence fell around the table. Here was a poker game that would make history on the Mississippi, that would be woven into the fables and songs of the black roustabouts. The story of this game would travel up the wild log rivers of Wisconsin and Minnesota, spread out over the Western plains, sweep along the crowded, busy levees of St. Louis.

Young Tom Connally was leaning forward, poised in eager challenge on the edge of his seat.

Matt Jordan sat motionlessly. He was grave now, save for the slight flicker of admiration in the glance he sent across the table.

Before Matt could speak, the smoking-room door burst open. The neat, gray-haired figure of Captain Smithson came straight to the card table. The captain was agitated.

"Mister Jordan, your raftsmen are out of control! Two bullets have cut through the cabin floor, frightening the ladies!"

"Only part of them are my raftsmen, Captain. I merely pay their passage back upriver, you know."

"They've clubbed my mate unconscious," the captain said angrily. "There are sixty men down there armed with guns and knives and wild on whiskey. They're threatening to move up here on the cabin deck and take over the boat. Can't you do something with your men?"

Matt pushed back his chair and stood up. "I like your

offer," he said to Connally. "It's sporting enough. If you will wait until I step below, we'll show our cards. Your Bank City sawmill or nothing."

Matt put his cards face down on the table. He was a big, loose-moving figure, grave and intent as he walked to the barroom door.

At the door, he turned. His voice was low and vibrant. "I suggest, gentlemen, that no man on this deck fire a gun unless necessary. The raftsmen are hot-headed, you know."

Uneasy knots of passengers were gathered in the brightly lighted main cabin. As Matt entered, the pandemonium on the lower deck sounded louder, surging up the wide stairs. Matt ran his grave glance over the passengers. He said quietly: "It might be better if the ladies went to their rooms."

Matt was not surprised that his answer came from the slender blonde girl who had come aboard at the St. Louis levee. Then, in the soft, white sunlight, she had seemed like laughter and flame. She had been vividly alive in every movement, every play of expression on her oval face. A dollar in the eager hand of a black cabin boy had fetched him her name before the lines were cast off at St. Louis. She was Miss Matha Vickers. The tall, erect, bearded man who had accompanied her and another young lady aboard was Judge Vickers of St. Louis, her uncle. And the black-haired beauty with Miss Vickers and her uncle was Miss Althea Temple.

Matha Vickers was with her uncle now in the main cabin. Her voice rose clearly, slightly scornful in reply to Matt's proposal: "You might better suggest, sir, that there are enough gentlemen on board to stop the drunken rioting below. It's . . . it's outrageous."

"It's mostly bad whiskey and rough men, ma'am," Matt

said calmly. "I'm afraid gentlemen aren't what's needed to stop it."

The easy laughter of Tom Connally came at Matt's shoulder. "Matha, I've always insisted there were drawbacks to being a gentleman. Since there's doubt, watch what happens to two gentlemen now."

Connally had followed Matt out of the barroom. Others were now straggling forth, most of them uneasy, plainly fearful of what might happen in the next few minutes. Men were running about on the freight deck. The boat quivered under the pound of their heavy-booted feet. A roustabout's wail of terror cut short abruptly.

A wild, wolf-like howl of drunken humor wafted up the stairs. "There's another 'un hidin' behind them boxes o' freight!"

Matt turned to the stairs. Connally moved along at his side. "Keep back," Matt said.

"Wouldn't think of it, suh."

"You'll do no good."

"I'm a bit light . . . but I'm fast."

"Don't be a fool," Matt said roughly. His weather-darkened face had tightened, so that ridges of muscle lifted along the line of his jaw. In some vague, indefinite way he had changed from the musing, intent man who had sat hour after hour at the card table.

Connally gave him a puzzled look, and then protested: "I can't let you go down there and have all the sport alone. Never respect myself afterwards, suh."

The winning smile, a black eyebrow lifted in challenge, brought no approval to Matt's stern look. "You don't understand," he told Connally. "They'd gang up on you and think it a joke." Matt hesitated on the top step, at a loss for the right word. "They don't like gentlemen," he said in blunt truth. "I've got enough on my hands without having to worry about you."

A cry of fright, a scramble of running feet—and a terrified roustabout bolted up the stairs toward the forbidden territory of the cabins.

"Dey gonna kill me! He'p me, white folks!"

After the fugitive came a shouting stampede of big, roughly dressed men in slouch hats and woods caps. Some had clubs, some guns and knives.

The terrified roustabout stumbled. Matt caught him by a shoulder and pushed him on up the steps.

"Hide him, Connally," Matt said in a clear, hard voice.

Matt descended two steps with lithe movement. Knees slightly bent, broad shoulders hunched, he waited.

The leader of the pursuit had an old black hat far back on his head. His heavy black mustache framed broad, thick lips, his shirt sleeves were rolled up, and he carried a short heavy club.

He stopped below Matt, and the others crowded up behind him.

"Ef it ain't big Matt Jordan!" the leader said, breathing hard. "Git outta the way, Matt! We aim to teach that boy manners!"

"You're Tige Ellis, off the Black River," Matt guessed. "Back from a Bixby and Smith raft to Saint Louis."

"You know dern' well who I am, Jordan! Git outta the way!"

"I've heard about you," Matt said. His gaze ran over the other excited, upturned faces—settled on one near the bottom of the stairs. "Long John! What's all this about?"

Long John towered half a head above those around him. A black woods cap was cocked jauntily on one side of his shock of red hair. His face was covered by a flaming, uncombed red beard.

"Ain't nothin' much," Long John answered. "There's been some fightin' an' target shootin', that's all. Some of the boys got riled by the roustabouts."

"I'm not hiring men who'll be led into trouble by a Black River drifter like Tige Ellis. Get the Jordan and Wheat men back to the main deck and sobered up. That is, all you can whip. I'll take care of the rest."

Tige Ellis lifted the club. "Ain't no man calls me names and walks away from it!"

"Get back down on the freight deck and I'll oblige you," Matt said briefly.

"Fight!" one of the men yelled. The cry was taken up: "Fight! Tige Ellis an' Big Matt Jordan from the Waymego River!"

"You comin' down from your fancy roost to fight me?" Tige Ellis demanded.

"I'm coming down to whip you," Matt said. He spoke to the others: "Will you feel like sleeping it off after you see Ellis whipped?"

Laughter and jeering assent answered the question. "I'd snore like a baby ef I seen a fight like that!" called one big bearded man. The stairs shook as they jostled and pushed back down.

Matt did not look back at the cabin passengers who had moved cautiously near the stairs. The freight deck was dark at the bow, with the river close underfoot, gurgling, rushing back as the great sidewheels drove against the current.

Matt kept close behind the broad shoulders of Tige Ellis. A lantern glowed in a clear space among the freight. Shadowy forms clambered to vantage points on hogsheads, crates, and boxes.

Tige Ellis whirled without warning and struck with the

18

club. Matt had been watching for something like that. He was not caught off guard. He leaped in close, and the club missed him. Ellis's weight went off balance against him.

Matt's hands came up together, slightly cupped, with terrific force. The hard palms hit the sides of Ellis's jaw and drove the big man's head back so violently it seemed bone must snap. The blow lifted Ellis off the floor and he pitched back full-length on the rough deck boards.

A howl went up from the intent watchers. "Stomp him, Matt! Stomp him!"

Ellis scrambled up and shook his head. Shaggy hair was over his eyes as, with outstretched arms and lowered head, he rammed at Matt's middle.

Matt dodged and turned slightly. His knee smashed up into Ellis's down-turned face. The big man stumbled and clutched wildly at Matt's hips. Ellis hung on, hauling himself upright against Matt's body. He was bleeding from nose and lips smashed by the knee.

Matt hit him in the face. Ellis's arms tightened like straining cables. He stomped Matt's foot and wrestled close, bending Matt back.

"Tige's got him now! Tige'll bust his ribs an' back an' stomp him to mush!"

In the flickering lantern light Ellis's face was a bloody, grinning mask of triumph. Matt felt his ribs compressing, his back bowing in. He had both hands against Ellis's chest. He moved them up toward the throat.

Tige Ellis guessed the intention, thrust his head over Matt's shoulder so his throat was protected. His massive arms increased the crushing pressure. He threw his full weight hard forward.

Matt dropped back suddenly, bringing up his knees. He fell under Ellis's weight, to a partially sitting position, instead of flat back into helplessness on the deck. He rolled backward with an explosion of constricted muscles that carried Tige Ellis headfirst over on top of him.

Startled by the unexpected ending to fighting routine that had always worked before, Ellis let go, hurtling on over into a scrambling heap. They came up together and Matt struck the bloody face so hard Ellis reeled back against the stacked freight boxes. What had been grim, slow-moving, and deadly was suddenly breath-catching action, no less deadly.

Ellis bounced off the packing cases, spitting blood and oaths. Another smashing blow drove him back. He was still against the freight boxes when Matt closed in, striking faster than most eyes could follow in the murky gloom.

Big hard fists smashed Ellis's head back against the wooden cases again and again. Ellis tried to shield his face behind his massive arms. Looping blows knocked him upright again. He bellowed through crushed lips. He tried to duck. Each time a blow straightened him up. Once more he tried to rush.

Matt let him come two steps. He dropped into a crouch and caught the man around the middle. He heaved him off the floor. For an instant Matt staggered under the great, struggling weight. Then he hurled Tige Ellis head down on the rough deck planks. Ellis rolled over and lay limply.

Gasping, Matt turned away. The smile came back to his sweating face. "That enough to turn in on, boys?" he asked.

They yelled with delight, swarming down off the stacked freight. Peace lay over the freight deck when Matt walked back up the cabin stairs alone.

He was disheveled and soiled, and a great weariness filled him. A wet bandanna handkerchief had wiped blood off his bruised knuckles, but the marks of the hard fight were on him as he walked up into view of his fellow passengers.

A murmur of comment ran among the men and women. Matt's glance came to rest on Matha Vickers, standing with the Temple woman. Matha was pale. Matt's look brought a wave of red to her cheeks, but she did not look away. Her eyes were estimating him when Thomas Connally joined him eagerly.

"Are you all right, suh?"

"I've been in worse shape. But I've had about enough for tonight. I'll be agreeable to calling off the card game if you like."

Connally stiffened, then smiled. "I choose to think you are not trying to spare me losses which I invited, suh. We've made the bet and have only to show our cards. I hold a straight, suh, jack high."

"I had a straight, too . . . queen high," Matt said calmly. "You'll look at my cards, of course."

Ever after he would remember the clear hazel eyes, not so excited now, that met his look. There was defeat in them, but it was good-natured, without envy or regret.

"It couldn't happen again in a lifetime," Connally said, clapping him on the shoulder. "My congratulations, suh. You've won a fine sawmill in Bank City, in good condition and operating at a profit. I guarantee it. While we are cashing in the game, I'll have my signature witnessed by the bartender. If you care for a more legal bill of sale, we'll see a lawyer tonight or tomorrow in Bank City. You will get off at Bank City, I suppose, to see your new property."

Matt nodded. "I could wish I'd won it from someone less a gentleman," he said.

"That pleases me, suh. Don't give it a thought."

Connally put out his hand. Matt shook it. Together they

went into the barroom to inspect the cards, cash in the game, and have a final drink at the bar.

II

In his small cabin Matthew Jordan wrote a letter to his partner, Sam Wheat:

Dear Sam:
   I have risked our capital and won a sawmill. I was a fool and had the luck of a fool. It should teach me a lesson. Twice a fool will not bring twice the luck.
   Well, Sam, we have our first sawmill now. This night's work puts us two or three years ahead of our plans. I am going to get off the *Silver Eagle* **at Bank City and see what saw capacity we have. It might be wise to have a raft of logs stop at the mill in case they are needed. I will give this letter to Long John to carry to you.**
                              Your partner,
                              Matthew Jordan
   P.S. I am still a fool for risking our capital and will expect to be treated accordingly when we meet.

Matt put the letter in his pocket and packed his worn carpetbag. He wiped his face, combed his hair carefully, and with a towel slapped off all dust and dirt from his dark rough-weave suit.

He paid no attention to the admiring interest of the passengers as he crossed the main cabin and descended to the freight deck.

Long John towered above him as they walked together in the dark bow. The big red-bearded raftsman laughed deeply in his throat. "Ain't gonna be no more trouble tonight. They poured water on Ellis for five minutes before he come to."

"I was afraid he'd hurt his head."

"You only left him meaner than ever," Long John said under his breath. "Don't be surprised if a knife hunts your back some dark night. Ellis ain't a man to forget. He's kilt before . . . an' he'll do it again."

"I'll be watching for him," Matt said. "Keep your men quiet the rest of the trip if you can, John. The raftsmen are getting a worse name every year along the river."

"I ain't seen nary angel ever working a raft downriver." Long John's voice shaded off into elaborate disinterest. "There's talk come down from the barroom that somebody won a sawmill in a big poker game tonight."

"I'm getting off at Bank City to look at it," Matt said. "Give this letter to Sam Wheat. Then get set for some hard work, John. Sam and I will be operating bigger than Bixby and Smith before long."

"And after that there's no telling, huh?"

"No telling," Matt agreed.

Muscles were protesting, bones aching as Matt went back up the stairs. He knew, better perhaps than anyone who had witnessed the fight, how close he had come to disaster down there on the freight deck. Tige Ellis had a reputation as a fighter, and he made a point of crippling any man he whipped.

He wanted no more of the barroom. Whiskey was a pallid substitute for the elation that bubbled in his pulses. The years had advanced suddenly, now that Sam Wheat and Matt Jordan had their first sawmill. Plans that had been buried in the distant future were now at hand. Dreams that had been only dreams could now be shaped into realities.

Althea Temple was sitting alone in the main cabin. Matt walked up to the texas deck, where the stars hung brightly overhead and the broad sweep of the river stretched out on either side. Because of the slight mist, the cool wind, and the lateness of the hour, not more than two or three passengers were out on deck. Matt paced slowly along one side of the deck and back along the other, and, when he saw a slender figure in cloak and bonnet ahead at the rail, his steps slowed and stopped.

He saw the small, bonneted head turn curiously toward him. He bit off the end of his cigar and risked the pilot's displeasure by igniting a match and holding it to the cigar, so that his face was briefly visible. He paused again when he came abreast of the girl.

"It's a pleasant night, isn't it, ma'am?" he said politely.

She turned her head, and in the starlit night Matt once more was deeply, fully aware of her direct and estimating gaze.

"I find it more pleasant than it was," she said coolly. "Did you find it necessary to go down among those ruffians and brawl with them . . . or did you enjoy it?"

Matt chuckled softly and faced the rail beside her. "I would value your opinion on the matter, ma'am."

She said: "I believe you enjoyed it."

"I wondered if you didn't think so," Matt said calmly. "That's why I hoped I'd find you up here."

"You followed me, sir?"

"No, ma'am. But I would have, if necessary."

The saucy bonnet shadowed her face; he could only guess at her expression by the stiff set of her small shoulders.

"Why would you have followed me?" she asked, looking out over the quiet river.

"Because you didn't seem to understand, ma'am, that there were almost seventy armed men going wild down there."

"Part of them in your employ, Mister Jordan. I suppose that is why you felt it necessary to brawl with them."

"I felt it necessary to stop them," Matt said patiently.

Before she could speak again, the great whistle burst deafeningly above their heads. And then, with the echoes still in their ears, they heard fainter shouts, oaths out on the water.

"Keep off! Keep off! Ye double-damned river hog! Keep off afore we shoot!"

"Another log raft," Matt said, and he laughed softly. "They don't like a steamboat's wash. It breaks up a raft sometimes."

Like a monstrous rectangular pancake, the raft slipped past in the night, fully 350 feet long.

They could barely make out men at the great sweeps. But they could hear the shouted, angry oaths of the raft's crew as the steamboat passed too close to suit.

"Is it one of your rafts?" Matha Vickers asked.

"No," Matt said. "But there'll be many rafts of mine come down this river before I'm through."

He fell silent, chewing the cigar. He saw the quick, steady look Matha Vickers gave him, and he stared upstream.

"There're forests standing ahead of us, ma'am," he said slowly, "that have lumber enough to build houses for the whole earth. It's an empire of soft pine such as the world has never known."

Matha Vickers sounded amused. "Aren't you being a

little lyrical about mere trees, Mister Jordan? One sees trees everywhere."

"Not like this sawmill pine, ma'am. Not with the woods rivers flowing to the Mississippi and the plains lying there to the west of us."

"The plains, sir, have no trees."

"Exactly," Matt agreed. "No trees. Millions of acres of the richest farmland on earth. The settlers are coming faster each year. The railroads are pushing West. This is Eighteen Fifty-Six, ma'am. Within my lifetime and yours we will see fences where the buffalo graze, and towns and cities where the Indians now camp. Remember what I tell you. And there are no trees on those plains."

"I think I see what you mean," Matha said slowly.

Matt leaned lightly against the rail, looking up the river through the cool mist that flowed about their faces. His quiet, musing voice had a soft strength of which he was unconscious. "The pine lumber for those towns and cities and farmhouses and railroad ties and furniture will have to be carried to the plains." Matt flung out an arm toward the north. "There are the pine trees and the rivers to bring them down. Not in rafted lumber from the little mills along the banks, but as they are starting to do now, in logs to the bigger mills. I'd rather have sawmills in Saint Louis, near the mouth of the Missouri, than gold mines in California." He struck the rail lightly with a clenched fist. "And I will!" he said.

Matha Vickers was looking at him with an unfathomable expression. "Other men may have had the same thoughts, Mister Jordan."

"I know some of them," Matt agreed. "It's going to be dog eat dog." He knocked the ash from his cigar. "I've got a good appetite, ma'am, and so has my partner."

Matha was not amused. Her manner had a strange, cool reserve. "Tonight you took one bone away from a smaller dog. A weaker dog, shall we say, who probably never in his charming life thought much about cities yet to be built on the Western plains."

Matt looked at her with a quick withdrawing into guardedness. "I risked everything my partner and I had built up in eight years, ma'am. I sat in a small poker game and saw it get larger against my wish. I could have lost, and no one would have felt sorry for me . . . least of all, the gentleman of whom you speak."

"Tom Connally has never had to be sorry. He was born to what he has and more that he has lost," Matha said calmly. "It has been enough for him to be a gallant gentleman aware of his weaknesses."

"I've never been able to afford the luxury of weakness," Matt said dryly.

"I believe you," Matha said. "You are strong, Mister Jordan." She turned away from the rail, adjusting the cloak. "Take care, sir," she said, "that you don't meet stronger men."

Matt watched her leave him. The deck trembled to the steady drive of the engines, the monotonous thresh of the big paddle wheels. A fantail of crimson sparks spewed from the high twin smokestacks and vanished astern. The river was broad, quiet, and suddenly very lonely. Matt threw his cigar over the rail and walked forward, vaguely discontented.

The feeling passed, however, as he thought of Bank City, close ahead, and the sawmill now owned by Jordan and Wheat. He felt no regret at having won the mill. The game had been honest. Connally had been a skillful player. A girl like Matha Vickers had no way of understanding men's business or pleasure, or the risks and rewards for which they fought and played.

The freight deck was still quiet. Above Matt's head voices were audible inside the open windows of the pilot house. A remark caught his interest.

"Yes, it's a big fire. I've been watching it for the last ten minutes. Ain't died down any."

Matt looked out through the night. Well to the right of the bow, above dark trees on the riverbank, the misty night had a faint reddish glow.

Looking up to the pilot's window, Matt asked: "What do you make of that fire? Patch of woodland or a farmhouse?"

"Neither one," the pilot's voice answered. "On a clear night it'd show much brighter. It's Bank City. Might be the whole town on fire, from the looks of it."

Matt remained on the top deck where he could see better. The pilot told him it would be an hour before the steamboat passed the big bend and the smaller bend ahead and reached Bank City. An hour was a long time to juggle uncertainty about the future.

People were stepping outside on the deck below and coming up on the texas to study the red glare that grew steadily brighter as distance diminished.

One of the professional gamblers stopped at Matt's side. "Well, sir," the man asked, looking at the red glow, "did you win a sawmill or a pile of hot ashes?"

"I'd like to know."

"It would make an interesting bet. Say, five thousand on it. Five thousand to you if the mill is not burning . . . five thousand to me if it is."

"No."

"You've been lucky so far tonight," the gambler persisted. His long, impassive face was familiar from other river trips; his name, Matt recalled, was Kram. "Your luck is probably holding, Mister Jordan," Kram urged. "It will be five thousand dollars easily won."

"Not interested."

"I think I'll step down to the barroom and suggest a wager to the former owner," Kram said easily. "He might appreciate the chance to win back a little."

Matt did not answer. The gambler left him. Half an hour later, from the rail of the texas deck, Matt watched in stony silence as his new hopes and plans were carried skyward in glowing embers, swirling sparks, and billowing clouds of smoke.

III

The sawmill itself had already burned. The fire was now in the great stacks of piled lumber about the building. As soon as he was certain that the mill had burned, Matt went below for his carpetbag. He was the first passenger down the stairs to the main deck, and there, while waiting for the *Silver Eagle* to make her landing, Matt spoke briefly to Long John.

"Tell Sam Wheat he'd better forget what's in the letter. I'm stopping here at Bank City to see what can be done to put the mill machinery back to work."

"Of all the sawmills along the river, it'd have to be this one," Long John said disconsolately. "It'll be many a day before you ever get another mill so easy."

"We'll get one," Matt promised. Connally had not appeared when Matt stepped ashore, first off the boat.

He knew that behind him, on freight deck and cabin

deck, he was leaving little sorrow and some amusement at this ending to the fabulous poker game. But that didn't bother him. There was still a chance that part of the mill machinery could be repaired and used again. Presumably the mill site still belonged to Jordan and Wheat. If not here at Bank City, then at some other site, they might yet saw logs years sooner than they had planned.

The mill was at the edge of town, with houses close to it. Three of the houses had already burned. Bucket lines were passing water to every roof in danger from sparks that still rained down.

Most of the town seemed on hand. Matt asked one group of men close to the withering heat of the burning lumberyard: "What happened?"

A bearded oldster answered him succinctly: "She caught fire couple hours ago. No telling how it started. Ain't no doubt how it's ended. We ain't got a sawmill no more."

The mill itself was smoldering débris. Saw rig, pulleys, and all metal parts had fallen into the glowing inferno of collapsed floors and walls. Metal parts were still red-hot. The boiler and engines stood, naked and forlorn, amid the smoking destruction. It would be tomorrow before a man could guess what salvage was possible.

Matt retreated from the acrid smoke and savage heat. He looked among the gathered townspeople for Thomas Connally, but without success. However, he did see, with surprise and a pleased jump of his pulses, the dignified figure of Judge Vickers and the judge's niece.

The judge touched his hat with stiff politeness as Matt uncovered. Matha's acknowledgment was the barest. But her look was searching, as if she sought to read things on Matt's face that he was hiding.

He walked on, slapping his hat roughly back in place.

Matha Vickers had shown no regret over the burning of the mill, no wish to be friendly.

Matt walked back to the small frame hotel where he had left his carpetbag. The owner was waiting for him with a sealed envelope. "Boy brought this from the *Silver Eagle* just before she pulled out. "Matthew Jordan, Esquire," read the man, peering at the envelope. "That right?"

"I'm Matthew Jordan."

Matt took the envelope and opened it. Some minutes later he was still pondering, with a set and thoughtful face, the strange message in the envelope:

Dear Sir:

Please be assured of my good faith in giving you a bill of sale on a mill which already was burning. In order to rectify the unfortunate error, I take pleasure in sending to you by bearer a second bill of sale on my Southern Cross mill, in St. Louis. The Southern Cross is a somewhat more valuable property. You can adjust the difference with my St. Louis lawyers, Samuel Carson, Enoch Carson, and John Jones, if you so desire. I find I have no further use for the Southern Cross, anyway. You will hear from me in St. Louis, or earlier, as I have decided to continue upriver on the *Silver Eagle*.

Respectfully yours,
Thomas Connally

The bill of sale to the Southern Cross mill in St. Louis was duly witnessed.

"When is the next boat to Saint Louis?" Matt asked the hotel man.

"The *Daniel Simpson*'s due 'most any minute."

"I'll write a letter to go upriver on the next boat," Matt decided. "I'll not be staying with you tonight, after all." He wrote again to Sam Wheat.

Matt had left St. Louis regretfully. He returned with the eagerness of a man who recognizes that destiny is directing his course. Here was the throbbing heart of the coming Empire of the West. Already St. Louis had a population of more than 100,000.

The great stone warehouses along the levee side of Front Street gulped in and disgorged a rising flood of trade. Here a man could strike bold blows to shape his vision of the future. Matt pondered his plans as he rode a jostling hack to the hotel. He signed the register and walked out again without bothering to inspect his room.

His first stop was the firm of lawyers representing Thomas Connally. Mr. Enoch Carson sat at an old desk in a narrow, high-ceilinged room and read the bill of sale for the Southern Cross mill that Matt had handed him without comment.

The lawyer was a small, withered man with scant gray hair combed across a bulging forehead. Matt did not like him. A massive gold watch chain, a strutting flourish of politeness followed by a quick estimation of the visitor's rough-weave suit had resulted in a marked lack of interest. Here, said action plainer than words, was no profitable client. Without expression, Matt watched consternation grow on the pale, lean, thin-lipped face of the lawyer.

"I don't understand this," Carson said, looking up. His voice was high-pitched and querulous.

"Speaks for itself, doesn't it? I own the Southern Cross mill. Connally seemed to think I'd better let his lawyers know. There may be a difference in cash I'll pay over to him later."

"I still don't understand. Where is Mister Connally? He had no plans to sell the mill to you. As a matter of fact. . . ." Enoch Carson stopped and pressed his thin lips together.

"Connally went on upriver from Bank City on the *Silver Eagle.*" Matt leaned forward and took back the bill of sale. "I thought I'd better let you know in case anyone at the mill refuses to show me the books or take my orders. You'll be agreeable to that, I suppose?"

"You're going to take charge of the mill, Mister Jordan?"

"I am. Are there any legal matters or papers in your hands that I should know about?"

"The mill has its own office and safe," Carson said. Consternation still gripped him. The flourish of self-importance had given way to an uneasy dismay. He cleared his throat and smiled with an effort. "We hope, sir, you will call upon our services as needed."

"I'll decide that when I need a lawyer," Matt told him. He stood up. "When Connally comes back, he can find me at the New York House on Second Street. I want to see him."

Enoch Carson followed him to the door. "Your bill of sale should be left in our safe, sir."

"I'll take care of it," Matt said.

The next call Matt made was at a small, inconspicuous office on Second Street, where the iron dealers, the heavy grocers, and receiving and shipping houses were located. The sign above the doorway said **BENJAMIN PIKE AND SONS—LUMBER**.

A bookkeeper was at a wall desk in a small, dingy front room. From a room at the back a deep voice roared a greeting as Matt stepped in. "Great jumpin' catfish! I thought we got rid of you t'other day! Come in an' wet your whistle."

Heavy feet hit the back room floor with a *thump*. The

speaker rose from a creaky desk chair and thrust out a big
hand. He was a huge old man, bald and tanned on top of
his head, and dignified by a vast gray beard that swept
down over his chest.

"I came back to talk lumber," Matt said. He had to put
forth hard pressure to save his hand from being crushed by
the enormous fist that enveloped it.

"You're always talkin' lumber," Ben Pike accused.
"Worse than them four boys of mine. Get a drink down an'
let's forget lumber. There ain't no lumber on the market.
All you've got is logs, an' not many of them."

"I've got lumber," Matt said.

"Where?" Pike roared, swinging around with a whiskey
bottle in his hand. The humor in his lively eyes gave way to
keen interest.

"I own the Southern Cross mill, Ben. We can do more
than talk sawmill lumber now. I want you and your sons to
handle everything we saw."

Ben Pike set two whiskey glasses on his desk and poured
two drinks before he grunted with disappointment. "I
thought you had lumber to sell. All you've got is a mill . . .
an' I don't put much stock in that until I see proof."

"Here's the bill of sale."

Ben Pike let the drink rest unnoticed on the desk while
he looked at the paper. "You didn't have no mill when you
left here t'other day, Matt."

"I won it from Connally in a poker game."

Pike drained his glass. He sat back heavily in the creaky
chair and shook his head while Matt drank.

"I knew young Connally was a fool, but I never looked
for anything like this. The mill didn't cost you nothin',
then, but some card playin'?"

"That's all."

"You ain't got nothin' to worry about then," Ben Pike said philosophically. "You might find someone around town that'd take it off your hands for nothing."

"What are you trying to tell me, Ben?"

Ben Pike turned down one thick finger of a big hand. "You got a sawmill that'll cost you money." He turned down another finger. "Your mill's contracted to deliver more lumber than it'll saw." A third finger went down in relentless emphasis. "The Southern Cross ain't even got enough logs contracted for to make the lumber it's agreed to deliver under penalty." Pike closed his whole massive fist and struck the desk edge a warning smash. "The Southern Cross mill was hog-tied, hobbled, ham-strung, and 'most ready to be took over by its creditors. They'll take it from you as quick as they aimed to take it from young Connally. Only they won't be so generous with you. Connally wasn't a threat to them. Fellows like you are."

"How do you know so much?" Matt asked mildly.

"I been findin' out why I can't get lumber for my boys to sell," Pike rumbled. He ran thick fingers through his beard. "My boys kin sell lumber like a prairie fire on the loose. We been handlin' more lumber every year. We been shippin' farther an' farther from Saint Louis. New customers all the time. We were so busy selling and shipping we didn't notice that mills were being bought up, saw output contracted for. When I finally smelled a rat and went lookin', the stink 'most knocked me over."

"Who's behind it?"

"I keep hearin' the names of Bart Bixby an' Kirby Smith."

Matt looked surprised. "They've been logging on the Black River and busy with rafting."

"That ain't all they been doing," Pike rumbled in his

35

great beard. "Bart Bixby comes from a good family. He's got powerful friends in Saint Louis."

Matt rubbed his chin. "Bart Bixby and his partner have been logging hard on the Black River. I've heard talk they're riding roughshod over smaller outfits that get in their way. We've had reports of their timber cruisers over near the Waymego, where Sam Wheat and I have been logging. I kind of thought we might be due to tangle one of these days."

"If you own the Southern Cross mill, you've already tangled."

Matt nodded. "Bart Bixby is smart."

"He's hard and heartless, too," Ben Pike growled. "See him over on Fourth Street driving a fine matched team, with a pretty girl at his side, and you'd think he was one of the local dandies. But tangle with him in business and he'll cut your throat while shaking your hand." Pike slammed his huge fist on the desk again. "I ain't sure Bixby ain't my friend even now . . . only I ain't gettin' lumber for my boys to sell, an' Bixby's crowd is doing the squeezin'."

Matt chuckled softly and stood up. "I'll go look at my sawmill. Sam Wheat and I don't scare easy. There's enough pine trees up north for everybody."

"Tell Bart Bixby that an' he'll laugh an' agree with you," Pike said sourly, going to the door with Matt. "An' then wait an' see what happens to you."

"It'll be a pleasure," Matt said.

IV

Matt drove a livery team out to Southern Cross mill. As he drew near, the keening shriek of saw teeth cutting

36

through green logs was music on the early afternoon air. He got out of the buggy in the mill yard, and stood for a minute looking about at the big, gaunt mill building, the great sawdust and slab piles, and the high stacks of green lumber. To his right, the Mississippi flowed tranquilly and logs waited inside the boom for their return to land and the shrieking saw teeth.

The boom was only a quarter filled with logs. It should have been full at this time of year. Matt was frowning at the sight when he saw Enoch Carson and another man come out of the mill office beyond the livery buggy. Matt stepped past the horse's head and did not miss the little lawyer's start of surprise at sight of him.

Carson and the man with him came forward.

"This is John Wing, your mill manager," Carson said when they met. The little lawyer blinked and cleared his throat. "I judged it advisable to inform Wing of the change in ownership."

"Kind of you," Matt said noncommittally.

Wing grinned and shifted a chew of tobacco to the other cheek. He was a gaunt, stolid-looking man in a rusty black coat and trousers powdered liberally with sawdust.

"I guess it don't matter who's boss so long as I get logs sawed," Wing said. "But it was sure a surprise to hear the mill had been sold. I guess you want to look around."

"I'll look at the books first," Matt said.

Hours later, when the shrill mill whistle blew and the machinery slowed to silence, Matt was still in the small office poring over books and records. He had said little to the middle-aged clerk who had hovered around uneasily all afternoon.

"Put these ledgers in the safe." Matt said. He stepped to the window and looked gravely at the employees hurrying

37

toward their homes. His men now. His mill. And problems he had not suspected confronted him at every turn.

Matt did not move as his eyes followed an open-topped buggy turning smartly into the mill yard behind a spirited pair of matched bay horses. But he could feel the driving warmth of interest as he recognized Matha Vickers beside the young man who held the reins with careless skill.

"Who is that man driving the buggy?" Matt asked.

The bookkeeper stepped quickly to the window. "Mister Bixby," he said.

Matt started to ask another question, then stepped outside without speaking.

Matha Vickers was surprised to see him. She said something quickly under her breath to Bart Bixby. Matt had time only to notice the added color coming into her cheeks and her gaze turned deliberately away from him. Then, as the smart team and buggy whirled around to a stop in front of the mill office, Matt gave his attention to Bixby.

Their paths had never crossed directly. The Bixby of north woods talk did not fit this sinewy, finely dressed gallant of the metropolis. Bart Bixby would be at ease in any drawing room. He stepped lightly from the buggy. He was only a shade under Matt's height, but somewhat heavier, all free, flowing muscle. He was clean-shaven and smilingly assured as he offered his hand.

"This is a surprise," he said. "I'm told you are the Matthew Jordan who has been logging on the Waymego. I'm Bart Bixby."

Matt shook the hand, feeling a bit awkward as he matched Bixby's smile. "My partner and I have heard of you, Bixby. I was meaning to talk with you in the morning about matters concerning the mill here."

Bart Bixby lifted his eyebrows. "I understand you now

own Connally's Bank City mill. Is there some connection with this property?"

"I own this mill," Matt said.

He heard Matha Vickers's gasp of surprise, but his eyes did not leave Bart Bixby's face, which showed disbelief, chagrin, then flushed with a quick, dangerous tide of temper.

"I hadn't heard," Bixby said. "Would you mind telling me the circumstances?"

"Connally can explain if he cares to," Matt said. "I've shown the bill of sale to his lawyers, if you want to question them. I've already taken charge here."

Matha Vickers's low, unsteady voice addressed him from the buggy seat. "So your appetite did not stop at murder, Mister Jordan?" she said.

"I don't understand you, ma'am. I've not murdered anyone."

"Not legally, I suppose," Matha said in a scornful voice. "But morally, Mister Jordan. You're cold, greedy, and cruel."

"This is unfortunate and not necessary," Bart Bixby broke in hurriedly.

Matt's gesture asked him to keep out. "I'll give you the pleasure of talking murder to Connally when he returns to Saint Louis," he told the girl calmly.

"I wish you the satisfaction of looking at his face and remembering what you've done, if God grants his return to Saint Louis," Matha said coldly. "The boat we took downriver from Bank City brought word that Tom Connally had jumped overboard from the *Silver Eagle* during the night. They were unable to find his body."

The mill watchman was on duty for the night when Matt

left the office. Matt had sent the manager and bookkeeper home and had stayed alone. But his mind had not been on figures and records.

The friendly, handsome face of Tom Connally had been there in the office with him, and the stiff, cold set of Matha Vickers's small shoulders as Bart Bixby drove her away. Matt's harsh protest had been for his ears alone in the small office.

"I could not have caught Connally and given the bill of sale back to him if I'd tried! I'd never have suggested he turn this mill over to me!"

Matt Jordan knew that. Sam Wheat would believe it. No one else would. Bart Bixby obviously hadn't. Matha Vickers's shaking scorn had put into words what others would accept as the truth.

Twilight was fast turning into night as Matt drove out of the mill yard. The mournful blast of a steamboat whistle on the river made him think again of Tom Connally's lifeless body.

"What's done is done," Matt said bitterly, aloud. "Let them think what they care. Sam and I will saw logs as Connally intended."

The moody, bitter decision stayed with him back to the livery barn.

It was full dark, sable-black before moonrise, as Matt walked toward the hotel, conscious that he was ravenously hungry.

He gave no thought to the dark alley mouth down the street from the livery barn. He had almost passed the inky opening when his senses, finely tuned to lonely woods trails, cried warning at a stir of movement in the shadows.

Swinging fast, Matt caught sight of a lunging figure almost on him. As he tried to dodge, he took the crushing blow of a club on a shoulder. He struck wildly at his assailant, and heard the man grunt. Too late Matt realized he should have run. Two more figures had materialized out of the murky shadows. They had him surrounded, trapped. Then, from behind, something struck him on the head. . . .

A beam of clear warm sunlight brightened the barewalled room where Matt opened his eyes. He was in bed with a thick swathe of bandages about his chest and other bandages on his left shoulder.

It took a little effort to realize that this must be a hospital, and this was another day. His head and his side hurt when he moved. He discovered that his head was bandaged. When he tried to sit up, the bare walls danced crazily, and weakness made him glad to drop back on the pillow.

Matt was fingering the day-old stubble on his face when a kindly bearded face looked in the doorway, noted the open eyes, and came into the room.

"Good!" the stranger exclaimed with satisfaction. "You feel better now?"

Matt struggled up. "Where am I? How long have I been here?"

"Good," said the bearded stranger again. "Sometimes they die, sometimes they are thick-headed and want to run home quickly." He chuckled. "You are thick-headed. I am Doctor Gerhart. You are in the hospital. Also, you are a sick man, Mister Jordan, and should lie back. Your shoulder is dislocated, your scalp cut, and you have a knife wound in the side."

Matt was glad to lie back. "This is the next day?"

"The next afternoon," the doctor said, reaching for

41

Matt's pulse. "The attack on you was seen from across the street. Help arrived as you were being dragged into an alley. The men ran away. It is not known who they were."

"Where are my clothes? I had some papers that may have been stolen."

"I think not," said Dr. Gerhart. "Your wallet is missing, but we found a paper in a hidden pocket, a bill of sale to a sawmill. It is locked up. You have had visitors, since an account of the attack was printed in the newspaper today. A gentleman by the name of Benjamin Pike, and a young lady. Both said they would return."

Matt nodded and winced as pain rolled around in his head. "Keep that bill of sale safe," he muttered.

After the doctor left, Matt tried to put the facts together. His wallet was gone, but that was no great loss.

Robbery of a stranger could have been sufficient reason for the attack. But the three men had been unnecessarily savage. By the doctor's account they had tried to drag him into the alley. Matt wondered what else could have been behind the attack. He fell asleep thinking about it.

Ben Pike was sitting in the room when he awoke several hours later. "Glad to see you, Ben," Matt said, sitting up against the pillow. He felt stronger.

The old man stood up and towered beside the bed. "You oughta be." Pike's glance was straight and sharp with interrogation. "You still got that bill of sale to the mill?"

"Doctor Gerhart says it's locked up."

"I wondered."

"So did I." They looked at one another. "Bart Bixby drove out to the mill while I was there," Matt said. "He's a fire-eater."

"He's a rattlesnake," Pike growled. "Did you have any

misunderstanding with him?"

Matt shook his head and winced again at the jolt of pain. "Bixby was surprised to find I owned the mill. Any business we had together was left until another time." He frowned, remembering. "Connally jumped off the steamboat after I left it at Bank City. I seem to be held responsible for his death."

"I heard about that, too," Pike said. "News has a way of getting around town when the right folks want it spread. The poker game you an' Connally played and the way the Bank City mill was burning before you saw it are being told with the rest of the story. Nothing you can do about it, so you may as well forget it."

"Which means the talk says Connally would be alive if I hadn't stripped him in a poker game," Matt guessed.

"Talk never shaved no hairs off a skunk's back."

"But leaves him still a skunk," Matt said, smiling crookedly.

"Them who know you ain't thinkin' you're a skunk. The rest don't matter. I drove out to your sawmill. It's running as usual. You goin' to have any lumber for my boys to sell this year?"

"I'll see what we can do."

"My guess is you can't do enough," Ben Pike said. "My second guess is you'll keep trying. I thought that before you got outta bed it'd help to know Ben Pike and Sons are rootin' for you."

"It does help, Ben . . . now that I've got an idea what I'm up against."

"Helps us, too, to know someone else has hit town full of fight an' ginger," said Ben Pike. "Git you some rest now . . . an' don't leave here until you're fit for trouble. You'll probably find trouble quick."

Ben Pike had been gone an hour, and the sun was beginning to set, when an admiring hospital attendant ushered Althea Temple into the room.

Matt's astonishment was evidently written on his face, for Althea Temple laughed delightedly as she relaxed on the chair placed near the bed.

"Really, Mister Jordan, if it's dismay you're showing, it can't be helped. We've not been introduced, but I made bold to take the liberty. I'm Althea Temple. I was on the *Silver Eagle*."

She was unabashed and sure of herself, as only a girl could be who was worldly and wise about men. Her thick, finely textured black hair was a perfect frame for the flawless oval of her face. The expensive India shawl she dropped back off her shoulders gave full view of a slender, proud neck. A steady, graceful sureness was in each movement she made.

"I'd not be a man with eyes if I'd missed you on the *Silver Eagle*, ma'am," Matt said gallantly.

Gray-blue eyes under long lashes surveyed him with composed humor. "You're wondering why I'm here."

"I'm satisfied that you *are* here."

Althea Temple caught a red lip under even, white teeth and surveyed him thoughtfully. She leaned forward slightly as she spoke. "I've come to warn you that Bart Bixby takes anything he wants, Mister Jordan . . . whether it be sawmills, timber tracts, or a girl. I'm curious whether it matters what Bart takes from you."

"There's nothing but a sawmill he could try to take from me."

"I saw you look at Matha Vickers on the steamboat, Mister Jordan. I'm not blind . . . and I know Matha better than she knows herself." The gray-blue eyes darkened with

44

a shadow of bitterness. "Also, I know Bart Bixby."

"What are you trying to tell me, ma'am?" Matt asked.

V

Althea Temple's gray-blue eyes were intent as she sat by Matt's hospital bed. "I'm trying to warn you about Bart Bixby," she said evenly.

"Why?" Matt asked. His battered head still held waves of pain under the bandages. The knife wound in his side and the clubbed left shoulder were hurting. Weakness was making the bare white walls waver out of focus.

Althea Temple, leaning toward him, was like some gorgeous black-haired product of delirium that he could admire but not understand. With an effort he focused attention on the oval of her face and her cool explanations.

"Perhaps I'm sorry for you, Mister Jordan. Have you thought that Matha's uncle, Judge Vickers, can influence your affairs through his business connections? The judge could do much to help a close friend of Matha's."

Matt's strained smile sprang from dizziness that made the room dance. He had the whirling sensation that none of this was real. That lovely girl probably would vanish if he closed his eyes and opened them again. He tried it and she was still there.

"Tell Miss Vickers," he said with husky sarcasm, "that my heart was at her feet from the moment I saw her come on board the *Silver Eagle*. Tell her. . . ." Matt caught his breath at the pain in his head and the dizzy pit into which he seemed to be sinking. "Tell her," he mumbled, "there's no sunshine without her, no happiness unless she gives me hope and her uncle helps me."

"You're sick!" Althea Temple exclaimed with quick concern.

"Not too sick to wonder why you're here with such talk, ma'am."

Through his dizziness he watched Althea Temple hurry out for the attendant. She did not return, and she left a mystery as to why she had interested herself in his affairs.

Sam Wheat came down the river four days after Matt left the hospital. The sight of Sam's stocky, light-stepping figure crossing the mill yard sent a wave of relief through Matt.

They were not alike, but the indefinable cement of comradeship had bonded them closely during years of hard work. Sam's strong, weather-beaten face, spattered with irregular freckles, was one broad grin.

"What crazy business is this?" Sam demanded. He looked around at the mill property, then swung back, his grin broader. "You come here to Saint Louis for winter supplies, and then you start mailing sawmills to me."

"I played some poker," Matt said.

"Long John told me. He told me, too, how your man Connally jumped off the boat that night. I hear his body hasn't been found."

They had started to walk about the mill property as they talked. Sam's sideward glance noted the look on Matt's face.

"I still don't understand it, Sam. What else did Long John say about it?"

"Nobody seems to know much. Connally drank quite a bit in the barroom. Men who saw him said he seemed cheerful enough. About an hour upriver from Bank City a man named Kram reported that he thought someone had jumped off the texas deck. Kram wasn't positive. It was dark up there. Kram was standing on the other side of the texas deck. He didn't hear any sound, but he thought a shadowy figure had gone over the rail."

"Kram," Matt muttered. His face darkened as he recalled the tall, elegant gambler who had offered a $5,000 bet on the burning sawmill at Bank City.

"They checked the passenger list," Sam continued, "and turned the *Silver Eagle* back downriver when Connally wasn't found aboard. They didn't find him. He was probably smashed by the paddle wheel . . . . Look, Matt, I've got more curiosity than a buck antelope about how you got this sawmill."

"Connally sent me a bill of sale for it at Bank City before he went on upriver. He'd bet me a sawmill in first-class condition and he made good. There's a difference in value we're to pay to his lawyers when we see fit."

"So we've got a sawmill, finally. In Saint Louis, too."

"We've got enough headaches to swamp a timber raft," Matt said bluntly. "If we don't work fast, we may be back in the woods swinging timber axes for wages."

On the riverbank above the log boom, where the black, dripping pine logs inched slowly up the timber chute, Matt explained the troubles ahead. Sam's weather-beaten face lengthened.

"Might have known it was too good to be all true," he remarked. "So we've got a mill that hasn't been sawing what it should. And we're hog-tied with contracts and penalties to deliver more lumber than we'll have. The penalty is three hundred feet of clear boards free for each thousand we're shy at the end of the year. What kind of a contract is that?"

"Just the contract Connally would take a chance on signing," Matt said. "The bookkeeper has given me an idea how Connally planned. If the mill cut here at the Southern Cross wasn't enough, Connally intended to raft lumber from his Bank City mill. He was on his way to Bank City to start a lumber raft downriver when he sat in the poker game. He was going on upriver later to see about more logs."

"This late in the summer, with all the log cut out of the way," Sam snorted. "All that's coming downriver now are odds and ends and contracted logs for delivery before freeze-up. Why, it's near time to get the woods camps ready."

"Connally thought about all that . . . too late. There have been enough logs rafting down for open sale, so that he didn't worry. But this year something happened. Timber was contracted and bought before it arrived."

"Now Connally's troubles are at our door. What do we do?"

"Fill the contracts with Bixby and associates. That means more logs quick. I haven't told John Wing, the mill manager, to saw faster or get out. He's your problem."

"Mine?" Sam asked.

"You were raised in a sawmill, Sam. I'll get the timber out this winter. Did you start any logs this way?"

"Try and find logs that ain't contracted for."

"I'll have to . . . and lumber, too. And it's going to take money. Sam, we're short on capital. Each year we've been logging on a bigger scale and using all our profits. Now we've got to log still bigger, and saw here at the mill, too. Connally's bill of sale didn't include working capital. I've seen the bank. They'll give us an answer today about a loan."

48

Sam grumbled: "You'd think a free sawmill, some good timber rights, and the money from last season's log cut would be more than two river pigs like us could want. But all we seem to have is worry."

Matt ran his fingers absently through his blond hair. He looked out over the broad northward sweep of the river. "Will we ever get all we want, Sam? It's a big country, growing fast. You know all that we've planned. Not just one sawmill. A dozen big mills, if necessary. Not scattered timber tracts on the Waymego . . . but log camps wherever trees grow to cut."

"Big dreams . . . big headaches." Sam sighed. "Let's go bait that banker an' talk big money."

Sam Wheat would always look a little awkward out of calk boots and woods clothes. He was a man of the open, a man of hard-hitting strength and rough background. But Sam was not at all abashed as he accompanied Matt into the bank. Indeed, he walked with a swagger, as befitted a young timber man headed for greater things.

Mr. Fainwell, the vice president, received them with a hearty smile on a ruddy red-veined face. A man of cheerful dignity. Fainwell knew their account, on the bank books now for four years. He shook each warmly by the hand. And when they were seated in the small wainscoted office, Fainwell cleared his throat and smiled at them.

"I wish I had better news for you, gentlemen," he said. "Unfortunately . . . ."

Sam stiffened in his chair. "What news do you have, sir?"

"We'll not be able to make the loan you requested." Fainwell hesitated. "I'm sorry. At first I thought it might be possible."

Sam jumped up, anger darkening his face. "I wasn't here when Matt asked for this loan," he said, restraining his temper as well as he could. "But you know how we've been operating, sir. We've borrowed money before and paid it back. No one takes a risk when they give credit to Jordan and Wheat."

"I'm sorry, young man. There's nothing I can do. Judge Vickers, the head of our loan committee, was most positive the bank would not be able to handle your paper this year. Unless you can find a private banker, I'm afraid you'll have to go outside of Saint Louis in this matter, as you probably know."

"We know," Sam said.

Matt stood up. He was without visible emotion. "I didn't know Judge Vickers headed your loan committee."

"Since last winter."

"Thank you," Matt said. "Good day, sir."

Sam held in until they were outside. "I should have wrung that red-faced buzzard's neck," he said then. "We deserve a loan as quick as anyone else they deal with."

"We'll not get it. I could have told you so if I'd known Judge Vickers was on the loan committee."

"What's Vickers got to do with it?"

"He knew Connally well. He knows Bart Bixby even better."

"Bixby again!"

"Walk over and see Ben Pike," Matt suggested.

Sam's glance took in the fashionable carriages passing in the street, the fashionably dressed men and women. "I'd like to go on one hell-roaring drunk," he said, "an' see what kind of meat Saint Louis has got under the feathers. I been saving up a good bust for a long time now."

Matt gestured toward the next corner, where four ox-drawn prairie schooners were lumbering slowly across town toward the busy steamboat landings along the Mississippi levee. "More settlers for the plains," he said. "Next year they'll want lumber. Put off that bust for another ten years, Sam. You can bet Bart Bixby and his partner, Kirby Smith, are staying sober."

Sam's grin was infectious. "I can do it, too. But what a thirst I'll build up in ten years."

As Matt walked through the busy city streets after leaving his partner, he found his thoughts returning to Matha Vickers and the strange visit of Althea Temple to his hospital room. The Temple girl had hinted strongly of ties between Matha Vickers and Bart Bixby. Now Matt wondered with cold clarity how much influence Matha Vickers had exerted to shape the attitude of her uncle in the matter of the bank loan.

Since leaving the hospital, Matt had acquainted himself with the imposing brick residence of Judge Vickers, just around the corner from Fourth Street. He yielded to an impulse and turned off Fourth Street and rapped with the heavy knocker on Vickers's door.

VI

A neat Negro house man opened the door and bowed a white wool head in polite inquiry.

"Mister Matthew Jordan would like to see Judge Vickers."

"The judge, suh, is gone from town today, suh."

A cool, clear voice inside the house said: "Show the gentleman in, Columbus. I'll speak to him."

Matt stepped in with guarded wariness. The Negro took his hat and ushered him into a spacious parlor.

Today the bitter, scornful girl who had thrown Connally's death in his face was a self-possessed young lady.

"I didn't know you lived with your uncle, ma'am," Matt said lamely.

Slender, straight, lovely, in a full skirt of blue watered silk, with white lace over her small shoulders, Matha held his eyes. Her quick color showed awareness of his look.

"I have lived with my uncle for some years, Mister Jordan. Won't you sit down? I shall be pleased to give him any message you care to leave."

Matt lowered his weight carefully on a tapestry-covered small chair and looked at her thoughtfully.

"I had thought to protest the shutting off of my bank credit, evidently because of Mister Connally's death."

Once more Matt realized how direct and estimating Matha's look could be. She asked coolly: "What makes you think any decision my uncle made was influenced by Tom Connally's death?"

"What else could be the reason?" Matt said. "In a weak moment on the *Silver Eagle* I opened my heart to you about my future hopes and plans. Connally and I exchanged no words after you left me that night. He sent me a bill of sale to his Saint Louis mill after I had gone ashore. The steamboat was on its way upriver when I discovered what he had done. I could not have saved his life. But you are convinced that I was responsible for his death."

Matha adjusted her skirt. Added color was in her face. "I am betraying no confidence, Mister Jordan, when I tell you Tom Connally had nothing to do with your business at the bank. My uncle spoke of it to me. He considered the

Southern Cross mill a liability. He believes that Bart Bixby and other gentlemen associated with him will have you bankrupt in another year. You have no financial backing, insufficient experience, and have expanded too rapidly. My uncle decided it was too great a risk for the bank. Does that answer your complaint?"

"No. Because I don't agree with him. My partner and I won't go bankrupt. Bixby will be surprised if he's planning on it."

Matt stood up. He noticed the grace with which Matha rose. A ghost of a smile brought quick life to her face.

"I don't know that Bart Bixby is planning anything but hard work, Mister Jordan. He has already gone upriver to get his log camps ready. He plans, I believe, to spend all winter at his new logging headquarters in Belleville."

"Belleville?" Matt repeated sharply. "He's lumbering in the Belleville district this winter?"

"I believe so," Matha said. The slight smile curved her lips again. "On the *Silver Eagle*, Mister Jordan, I warned you to take care that you didn't meet a stronger man. I was thinking of Bart Bixby. As to your bank business"—Matha hesitated—"you needn't blame anyone. I took the liberty of urging my uncle to consider the loan carefully."

"You?" Matt said in astonishment. "I don't understand, ma'am. Why should you bother to speak for me?"

"Althea Temple brought me word from your hospital room that you wished my help," Matha said composedly. "Even on short acquaintance, I found it not difficult to do what kindness I could for an injured man."

Matt could feel the hot blood in his face as he recalled his feverish outburst to Althea Temple. The Temple woman was a vixen, and he could not guess what else she had told Matha.

"I'm sure I didn't mean to ask your help, but I'm grateful for it," he said, close to stammering. "This has been a pleasure, ma'am. I'll leave no message for your uncle."

Matha curtsied. He fancied she was laughing at him. Some way he got his hat from the black man's hand and left the house.

But the ordeal was not ended. An open carriage with a Negro driver was just pulling up before the house. Althea Temple gave him smiling recognition from under the ruffled edge of a pertly feminine yellow silk sunshade.

"How fortunate, Mister Jordan! I'm just in time to carry you where you're going."

Matt could do no more than approach the carriage, hat in hand. "Really, ma'am, it's not at all necessary."

The parlor windows were open and Althea called past him: "Matha, dear, I've changed my mind about stopping! I'll take Mister Jordan and see you later!" And with a gesture she indicated the seat beside her. "Do get in, sir. You're not up to walking so soon after leaving the hospital."

Matt clenched his jaw tightly on a sudden decision and got in. "I was going to the New York House, ma'am." And then he added coldly: "I find you've been unfairly indiscreet in repeating nonsense I babbled while sick in a hospital bed."

Althea's gray-blue eyes danced under the long black lashes. "I was sure you meant it," Althea said, unruffled and quite merry. "I knew Matha would want to hear what you asked me to tell her . . . and I couldn't help warning Bart Bixby that he must be on his guard against another suitor."

Matt sat motionlessly. "You have meddled unmercifully, ma'am," he said harshly. "You have probably turned a business rivalry into personal enmity."

"Bart did not seem too pleased," Althea admitted.

"You came to the hospital unasked and said you wanted to help me . . . although I'm still in the dark as to why. And immediately you hurried out to make me a laughingstock with Miss Vickers and an enemy to Bart Bixby. You've risked my future and my partner's future."

"Really, Mister Jordan, that was not my intention," she said, not smiling now. Her eyes under the heavy dark lashes filled with smoldering emotion. "I know Bart Bixby better than he knows himself. I know what I'm doing. Matha told me your plans, Mister Jordan. You want things that Bart Bixby wants, and both of you will fight for them."

"Yet you meddle," Matt said coldly.

"Why not, Mister Jordan? I've learned to fight for the things I want."

"What do you want?"

"I want Bart Bixby to meet a stronger man," Althea said. "I want him to know what it means to lose."

"In other words, you dislike Bixby, and you've picked me to pull your chestnuts out of the fire."

"Why, if you'll have it that way, yes," Althea agreed lightly. "You'll have to fight Bart Bixby to save yourself. And since you insist on scowling at me, I'd better tell you the rest."

"You've told me enough," Matt decided. "If you'll have your driver stop, I'll get out."

"My late husband," Althea said calmly, "was much older than I am, and his fortune was considerable. It would please me to lend you the money you need to fight Bart Bixby."

Matt looked at her with amazement that gave way to an impulse of dry humor.

"You are beyond comprehension," he said. "I'm glad I'm not Bart Bixby. We'll have no more of this meddling, ma'am, and you'll be free to keep your late husband's money for other purposes. I'll bring my own rafts downriver in my own way. And now I'll get out, please."

"I was afraid you'd be so foolish," Althea replied without offense. She ordered the driver to the curb. Once Matt got down, lifting his hat in stiff politeness, she smiled and said: "If you change your mind, Mister Jordan, I'll not have changed mine."

Matt was still angry as he walked into the lobby of the New York House. Sam Wheat was there with Ben Pike.

Sam stood up, grinning broadly. "Good news, Matt. Mister Pike says the bank's crazy and he'll prove it with his own money."

"I said I was crazy, too," Pike rumbled through his vast gray beard. "But if you can show me a way to come out in a knock-down fight, my boys an' me'll stay with you."

Matt sat down at the old man's left. "We've got a chance, Ben," he said. "But I'll warn you, it's a gamble."

"Let's hear it," said Ben Pike.

Some twenty minutes later, when Matt was through talking and answering questions, Ben Pike sat absently combing fingers through his patriarchal beard. "You got most of your log-camp supplies contracted for on credit and part of them already being shipped upriver," he said. "You've got a tidy sum of cash on hand from your last winter's log cut. You got timber tracts you can cut on for two years more. If you make good on your sawmill contracts, you'll come out owning the mill. All you need is bank backing to make sure you can handle your sawmill contracts and meet your log-camp expenses and raft costs next spring."

"That's all," Matt said.

Ben Pike's grunt was noncommittal. "But if you don't get clear of your sawmill contracts, the penalties will break you. And if you don't make a double cut of logs this winter and raft them successfully downriver, you won't have logs to saw and sell, for future operating expenses. You're on thin ice, boys. It won't take many mistakes or much bad luck to lick you."

"Sam can make a sawmill roll over and beg for more logs," Matt said. "I've got good men in the woods and I'll get the logs out."

Ben Pike heaved himself out of the chair. "You better, or we'll all be begging day work along the river. Come on over to the office and we'll get everything fixed up."

By late afternoon black roustabouts were rushing freight aboard the graceful steamboat Matt was taking upriver on quick notice. Next to it, a Missouri River steamboat had prairie schooners chocked on deck and lowing trail oxen forming background to buckskin-clad trappers and rudely dressed settlers.

Matt lingered on the levee with Sam Wheat and contemplated the prairie schooners. "More and more of them every year, Sam. The 'Forty-Niners were only the advance guard. They're going west from the river towns up north, too."

"Right now," Sam sighed, "all I've got on my mind is whether we'll keep our heads above water this next year. I'm keeping that John Wing on as mill manager. Haven't took his measure yet, but I'll get it soon."

"There's one thing I didn't tell Ben that you'd better know," Matt said. "Bixby and Smith have moved their logging headquarters to Belleville."

Sam ripped out an oath. "Hell, they're in our territory. I

knew those timber cruisers we spotted up the Waymego meant trouble."

"Bart Bixby's already gone north to the woods," Matt said. "But maybe there won't be any trouble. There's timber enough for everyone. You make the mill produce, Sam. I'll take care of the woods end."

"If I produce, I've got to have logs."

"You'll get logs before your boom is empty," Matt promised. "The cost may be high and no profit after they're sawed . . . but you'll get logs."

VII

Summer was fast drawing to a close when Matt went upriver. At Prairie du Chien, the oldest settlement on the upper river, almost 500 miles from St. Louis, Matt went ashore and waited two days for the small *Kitty Belle*, which made scheduled trips up the Wisconsin River until late fall. Raftsmen and lumberjacks, rivermen, traders, and trappers from the north crowded the busy little town.

Matt met the owners of two small sawmills up the Wisconsin River. His talk with them was a forerunner of many other talks he was to have with sawmill men up the Wisconsin and back down the Mississippi.

"You've been sawing all summer and you've probably got more lumber than the local trade can use. And extra logs that you can replace before freeze-up. I'll take all your first-grade lumber at a premium price, so long as you've got enough to make one crib. Cash on delivery and a good profit."

One of the mill men, from South Landing, said he could

make up two cribs of lumber and spare some logs.

An offer of double wages spread fast through town and had better results than Matt expected. When the small river steamer cast off and pointed up the Wisconsin, Matt had aboard two full raft crews and supplies. He arranged with the captain to stop at every sawmill up the river.

To each mill owner Matt made the same offer of quick profit for spare lumber and logs. At each mill where he bought a crib of lumber or logs, he dropped off men to construct the crib and went on.

It was simple to a man who knew rafting, logging, and the rivers. No one small local mill had enough lumber to consider rafting out. Matt's plan was to start far upriver with the first small lumber crib and add to it as the growing raft floated down.

He had four men and one raft pilot left when he supervised construction of the first crib at Moosetown. Below the small rough-boarded mill building they laid the sixteen-foot boards in criss-cross layers, twenty-four deep. Thirty-two feet long and sixteen wide the crib measured when they framed it in with pieces of two-by-eight, and bored the frame pieces with long wood augers and drove in grub-pin stakes to bind the frame.

That was the first crib. Matt saw it floating sluggishly down the river with a steering oar at each end, and he passed it half a day later on the riverboat carrying him downstream to the next small mill where a second crib should be waiting.

Logs, too, were bought and sent floating downstream to grow, stringer by stringer, until finally they followed Matt's progress down the Mississippi in large majestic rafts guided at each end by huge full-size sweeps.

Matt reached Prairie du Chien by steamboat ahead of

the first raft. He hired more men, arranged for full supplies
for the long Mississippi drift, and then continued downriver
by steamboat, bargaining for logs and lumber at the sawmills along the Mississippi banks. He worked far harder
than any of the rafting crews. Days slipped into weeks; the
scarlet and gold of frost-bitten leaves made glorious color
ashore and warned of the logging season in the north
woods.

The first raft of lumber and one of logs had already
reached St. Louis when Matt stepped off a steamboat at the
St. Louis levee. He had three hours to talk with Sam and
Ben Pike before taking the next steamer back upriver. He
had written ahead of his probable arrival, and he took a
hack first to the office of Ben Pike and Sons.

The drink Ben handed him tasted good, warmed and
spread the relaxed feeling.

"Sam can saw all winter if he's minded to now," Matt
said.

"Sam won't be here," Ben rumbled.

Matt sat up alertly. "Something happened to him?"

"He's going north with you. Got his things all ready."

"And leave some stranger to run the Southern Cross?
We can't do that."

"Who said a stranger? My two oldest boys is sawmill
men. I cleaned my teeth on a jack saw afore I was fifteen.
Ben Pike and Sons can run a mill, an' we ain't got nothin'
much to do these days anyway. I guess you ain't been
hearin' from your woods boss lately."

"I've been sending Long John orders by letter, but I
couldn't tell him where to catch me with any replies."

"He's been writing to Sam Wheat. Bixby and Smith are
going to give you hell on sled runners along the Waymego
this winter. And the way you've been spending money

upriver don't allow for extra hell and trouble."

"I had to spend it, Ben. What about Bixby and Smith?"

"Sam'll tell you on the boat. We ain't got time to go into all that now. The woods'll do Sam good. He's turned into a ladies' man."

"Sam's had his ups and downs with the ladies," Matt said with amusement. "The last one was Maggie, a six-foot waitress in a loggers' boarding house. She threw a pot of hot beans down his back and chased him out the door with a wet floor mop. Sam swore he'd never have another lady friend."

"He's made one and she ain't a six-foot waitress with a bean pot and dirty mop," Pike snorted. "She's got fine carriages an' finer clothes, an' there ain't a prettier woman in Saint Louis. She ain't Sam's girl, anyway, she's friendly to Sam because he's a friend of yours."

Matt jerked his head up quickly. "What's her name, Ben?"

"Missus Althea Temple," Pike said. "She sure must think a lot of you, Matt, the way she's been drivin' to the mill in her fine carriage an' askin' how you're gettin' along, an' invitin' Sam to her house for dinners an' introducin' him to her fancy friends. Sam has bought new clothes an' slicked up his hair. I seen him crook his finger the other day when he was drinkin' a mug of coffee."

"Sam's a fool!" Matt exploded.

By stage from Indian Town on the Mississippi to Belleville was some fifty miles over rough and dusty roads. With Matt and Sam Wheat in the stagecoach were two dance-hall girls, a lumberjack, a drummer traveling across state to Milwaukee, and a chunky French-Canadian with a good-natured flood of talk. Sam gained in spirits as the stage neared Belleville.

Belleville was at the big bend of the Waymego, a scant mile below Big Devil Rapids, six miles below Little Devil Rapids. Small steamboats from the Mississippi landed freight and passengers at Belleville on haphazard schedule. All the back country of the upper Waymego and tributaries used Belleville as the gateway out.

The Waymego pineries were hardly touched. Glacial drift, ponds, small lakes, and marshes, and the mighty blanket of close-ranked sawmill pine turned settlers to the rich prairie lands farther south. This was a Golconda awaiting double-bladed axes and sharp saws.

In late afternoon the pistol-like reports of the driver's long whiplash put the stage rolling, rocking in a dusty rush past slab and log shanties and the raw lumber buildings of Belleville.

The open bank of the Waymego River lay on the left; the merchants, saloons, and dance halls were on the right, facing the river. What little else was to Belleville straggled back to a belt of close-growing thickets.

The stage station was a small squared-log building next to Onion Hennessy's Tavern and dance hall. Matt and Sam picked up their carpetbags, which the driver had tossed down from the boot, and they set off along the broad plank walk.

Sam drank in the crisp air. "I've been needing a flannel shirt and calk boots. City life is too fancy." He caught Matt's look, and flushed. "I've told you twenty times I thought Missus Temple was an extra-good friend of yours."

Matt said: "Jordan and Wheat . . . logs, lumber, and tea parties."

"Cut it out. She was nice to me. What harm did it do?"

"I'd like to know," Matt said. He wheeled around as his name was called.

62

Long John hurried to them over the calk-gouged walk. A black woods cap was jauntily cocked, as usual, on Long John's shock of red hair. His free-flowing red beard had the same thrust of good-humored challenge, but Long John limped. When he came closer, they could see that one eye was puffed almost shut, an ear was lacerated and swollen. Long John carried all the signs of a terrific fight, even to bruised, swollen knuckles.

"I been watchin' every stage an' boat," he said with relief. "Seemed like you wasn't comin' north until snowfall."

"By the looks of you, it's a good thing we did." Matt chuckled. "Did you meet a bear?"

"Worse. Bixby an' Smith men." Long John spat. "I c'n walk. That's more'n some of our other men c'n do. That is, what men we've got left."

"So that's the way it is," Sam said with glassy mildness.

"Worse," said Long John gloomily. "I'm glad you two are here."

They turned right along another strip of plank and entered a slab-walled office divided into two rooms, each with a front window giving on the street.

The bookkeeper standing at a wall desk was slender, in his middle thirties. His face would have been pleasant if it had not been swollen on one side, bruised purple over the cheek bone.

"You too, Ike?" Matt commented.

Ike Bowman returned a lop-sided smile. "Looks like we can count on rough times ahead, Mister Jordan. Belleville's changed this fall."

"We'll change it back!" Sam said explosively.

Sam, roused to temper by what he had seen and more that he could guess, slammed his carpetbag into a corner and shouldered into the adjoining office room, muttering under his breath. Matt followed Long John in and closed the door, although the raw plank partition held cracks that precluded privacy.

Ten minutes later Sam Wheat was swearing mad.

"So it's a freeze-out before logging starts," he said furiously. "Reaching out for the best loggers with the best wages. Interfering with our supply teams, picking fights with our men."

"They haven't slowed us down too much," Long John said. "I ran the new logging road up Gopher Creek and put in a dam by that big rock Mister Jordan pointed out last spring. We've done a heap of cutting on tote roads. I've moved Camp One already. I'd rather you two made sure where we put Camps Two and Three. The men are staying at the old camps right now. That is, what men we've got."

"How do the men feel about it?" Matt questioned.

"Most of them have been with us before," Long John said dubiously. "They don't mind a little clean trouble. But if they've got to fight two against three or more whenever they step out of camp or come to town on pay day, I ain't sure what'll happen. A whipped-down outfit that's on the losing side don't help a man tie into his work an' grub like he should. An' when he can walk to a Bixby and Smith camp and get as good wages or better, I dunno. . . ."

Sam wheeled away from the dusty window through which he had been glowering. "I don't understand it, Matt. There's pine enough around here for a dozen outfits. Just because we've got a sawmill that Bixby an' Smith wanted . . . ?"

Matt leaned back from the board table that served as a desk. "It's more than a sawmill, Sam. It's looking ahead through the years. It's choking off threat of competition ten years from now. We've used a lot of our spare money. If our log cut is small and costs high, if we don't make the spring drive and raft runs to Saint Louis as planned, Jordan and Wheat will be like a rotten log ready for collapse. Long John, how many more men do we need?"

"Fifty or sixty, at least, including a good camp cook."

"Is Bart Bixby here in Belleville?"

"Him an' his partner. They've moved bag and baggage off the Black River."

"You go up to the camps and stay there," Matt decided. "Sam will be along in a day or so. And, Long John. . . ."

"Yes?"

"Dodge trouble all you can."

Long John gave him a queer look, but he made no comment before he limped out.

"Hell of a note. Dodge trouble. Get tramped on," Sam growled.

"We'd better start little and end up big," Matt said. "There should be men around Madison and along the Wisconsin River who haven't started for the woods yet. Get back on the stage before it leaves, Sam. Hire all the loggers you can get, up to a hundred. Offer fifty a month right through the winter if they'll work and fight for it. But make sure they're fifty-dollar men."

"We'll go broke paying wages like that."

"We'll go broke if we don't." Matt stood up. "Sam, you'd better get back to the stage station quick or you'll be left."

The stagecoach, with four fresh mules, pulled out a few minutes after Sam reached the station. Fifty yards down the dusty street the coach stopped as a man dashed out of a doorway and waved the driver down. There was a brief parley, and the stage rolled on with an additional passenger.

Matt stood on the plank walk and watched the stage out of sight. Something had been vaguely familiar about the burly stranger who had stopped the stage. Matt felt he should know the man but could not place him. With a shrug he turned into Onion Hennessy's Tavern and asked for his old room at the rear of the second floor.

Hennessy was a powerful Irishman with a head as bald and smooth as a peeled onion. "You going to be here all winter, Mister Jordan?" he asked as Matt signed the register.

"Why not?"

"Never can tell," Hennessy said. "Town's growed a lot this summer."

"What do the local folks think about it?"

Hennessy's gaze was noncommittal across the board counter. "They like it," he said. "The more big outfits we get logging up the Waymego, the faster the town'll grow. I already had to build an addition on the back."

"I can see your side of it," Matt said, equally noncommittal.

Matt was thoughtful as he left his carpetbag in the room and came back downstairs. Hennessy was a fair man and had given a fair answer. Belleville citizens were not taking sides this winter. Bixby and Smith money was as good as the Jordan and Wheat payroll.

VIII

Hennessy's Tavern was really two buildings connected. Hotel rooms and dining room in one half, saloon and dance hall and quarters for the dance-hall girls on the other side. A single narrow door, kept closed most of the time, gave access from the tavern office to the bar and dance hall. Matt stepped through and ordered bourbon whiskey. He stood at the end of the bar, his mind grappling with the identity of the stranger who had hurried to catch the stage. A vague feeling of uneasiness coupled with the memory.

The dance hall was quiet at this hour of the afternoon. Big Lena, the blonde Amazon who ruled the dance-hall girls with iron discipline, stopped at the bar end and said: "It's good to see you back, Mister Jordan."

"It's good to see you too, Lena." Matt meant it. "Have a drink?"

"You don't have to buy me drinks," Lena said reproachfully. She stood there by the bar, a big woman, almost six feet tall, nicely proportioned. Traces of a lusty, exuberant beauty were still evident under the powder and color on her face. Only her eyes were sad. Lena fingered the bracelets that loaded her wrists. Her dark eyes measured him. "It will be a hard winter," she said bluntly.

"Do you mean weather?"

"You know I don't," she said with a trace of asperity. Her ornate bracelets *clinked* softly on the bar wood as she turned to see where the bartender was standing. He was not near them. "You've been kind to me." She hesitated, seeking the right words. "You've treated me like a respectable woman. My girls hear things from these loggers. I tell you it will be a hard winter."

"I'm finding out," Matt agreed. "Was there anything in particular I ought to know?"

"I guess not. I'll tell you if there is."

"Thanks, Lena."

"You're a gentleman. I've only seen one other this summer."

"Who?"

Big Lena did not smile. The door had opened, and she was looking that way. "Not one of the men I see coming in. Be careful, Matt Jordan."

Matt's look grew intent as he moved toward the three men who had entered. With Bart Bixby and Tige Ellis was a loosely fat man, a stranger to Matt.

Bixby was not the handsomely dressed gallant of St. Louis. Calk boots, red-checked flannel shirt, black woods cap, and rough beard stubble gave him another personality. His quick smile had the mark of sincerity. "I heard you came on the stage, Jordan. Have a drink?"

"I just had one," Matt declined.

Tige Ellis was more primitive. His feelings were near the surface. Resentment showed in the big woodsman's look. Matt noticed a sizable scar weal at the corner of the heavy black mustache that framed Ellis's thick lips. His knee smashing into Ellis's mouth on the *Silver Eagle* had torn the lip and left the scar.

"Have you met my partner, Kirby Smith?" Bart Bixby asked easily.

"Dry weather we're having," Smith said morosely, not offering to shake hands.

He was fat over muscle. Folds of fat broadened his jowls and rolled loosely across his big middle. His dull brown eyes lacked expression.

Matt leaned casually against the bar, estimating the three. "My men seem to be having trouble with your crews, Bixby."

Bart Bixby put down his whiskey, drank water, and laughed easily. "Our Black River men get rough sometimes. They don't mean anything by it."

Matt smiled. "I like a little good clean fun myself," he said.

Leaving them, Matt had the feeling he was treading on crackling ice. He could sense three pairs of eyes following him out the swinging front doors. He recalled Matha Vickers's words on the upper deck of the *Silver Eagle* and in her uncle's parlor: *Take care you don't meet a stronger man . . . I was thinking of Bart Bixby, Mister Jordan.*

The recollection sparked deeply. Without her opinion he would have logged just as hard this winter. But because of it success would be sweeter.

Not until he was almost through supper that night did Matt recall why the stranger who had boarded the stagecoach seemed familiar. Matt left food on his plate when he quit the table a moment later. Across the small dining room of Onion Hennessy's Tavern he saw Bart Bixby glance up.

Twilight was somber, frosty, when Matt stepped into the general store of Isaac Peters. Tin-shaded coal-oil lamps shed dusty yellow light as Peters spoke across his counter.

"Fine to see you back, Mister Jordan."

"Thanks, Peters." With one quick look about the cluttered store, Matt had made sure they were alone. He came to the point immediately. "Who was the man who ran out of here this afternoon just in time to catch the Madison stage?"

Peters fingered his straw-colored mustache uncertainly. He was small, stooped, friendly with everyone.

"Seems to me his name is Pick," he said doubtfully. "Joe Pick. He works for Bixby and Smith."

"I was just curious," Matt said.

He was more than curious. Outside, in the swift swooping night, Matt cursed under his breath. The thing he remembered about Pick was the fast-plunging rush, like another rush that had come from the alley mouth in St. Louis.

Now he was certain beyond doubt that Pick was one of the three men who had clubbed and knifed him. Those three men in St. Louis had not been ordinary thieves. They had been waiting for Matt Jordan. Probably they had been after the bill of sale of the Southern Cross mill. They might or might not have had orders to kill their victim.

It was too late now to catch Sam, warn him. But then, reasoned Matt, Sam usually could take care of himself. In any event, Sam was on his own. The winter was just starting. There was time for a showdown before spring if one became necessary.

The next morning Matt left before daybreak for the log camps. A quickened sense of urgency went with him, coupled with bitter thoughts of Althea Temple in St. Louis. What was bad she had tried to make worse—and evidently had succeeded.

There was double work in the woods for every man on the payroll. Two camps to be shifted, along with horses and oxen, supplies and equipment. But that was the lightest work of all after Matt located the new campsites. The logging roads and tote roads were far from finished. New rollways were needed. Matt considered the dry, bright days and finally decided another dam was needed on Candy Creek above Camp Two. A dry winter would leave Camp Two's log cut rotting in a starved and shallow streambed unless a dammed back head of water swept the logs into the Waymego current.

Supplies brought to Belleville by the little shallow draft steamboats had to be freighted to the camps. But the greatest chore of all was the opening and smoothing of the log roads and tote roads through the virgin pine reaches.

First news of Sam Wheat came from half a dozen tall

Norwegian choppers who arrived by stage from Madison and were sent to Camp One by Ike Bowman.

Sam had picked good men and sent revolvers with two who had no guns. They stood outside the big log building that formed Camp One and told Matt they were ready to work or fight all winter.

Matt questioned them about Sam. They said he had had one hand bandaged when he hired them in Madison. Matt grinned with sober satisfaction. Sam had met Joe Pick and settled the matter in his own way.

A camp cook arrived, then day by day more loggers. Deep in the pines, riding saddle from camp to camp, Matt could follow Sam's progress in hiring men. When good ones were not to be found, he was hiring the rough ones, the hardcases. More than one man who came in was probably wanted by some sheriff. But they were all fighters and looked like good loggers.

Trouble with the Bixby and Smith men had stopped, strangely. Matt gave orders that the men stay around the camps on pay day nights and Sundays. Because summer inactivity was just past, there was little grumbling at first about the order.

Sam Wheat came back. He had been clear to Milwaukee where the plank roads were spreading out, railroads building, and sane and sober men sounded like drunks as they boasted of the rich years ahead from the Great Lakes to the Rockies.

"I caught that rascal sizing me up from the time he bolted into the stage at Belleville," Sam said in high spirits at the memory. "At that, he 'most fooled me. Went clean to Madison and didn't show his hand. But when I saw him following me to a tavern, I gave him a chance to get in his licks."

71

"What did you do?"

"Bought a set of brass knuckle dusters," Sam said, chortling at the memory. "Pretended to get drunk and walked out in a dark street. He came up behind me. When I turned, he jumped me. Almost broke my arm, too, before I could get him with the brass knuckles. I figured we were even."

"Did he admit Bixby had sent him?"

"I couldn't wait," Sam said. "The law was coming at a run. Besides, he couldn't talk. His jaw was busted and he was trying to run the other way. I brought the brass knuckles back. If I don't need 'em against Bixby's outfit, I'll need 'em around our own. I had to hire some hardcases, Matt."

"They're all right."

The camp foremen were old, experienced hands, and work had settled into a smooth routine. The Bixby and Smith camps already were logging farther up the Waymego. Belleville these days, when Matt went to town, was a peaceful community, poised for the inevitable onslaught of winter.

Ben Pike wrote from St. Louis that the mill cut was steady and large; contracts were being met. He told Matt not to worry about anything but getting logs out.

That lady friend paid me a visit, Ben wrote at the bottom of his letter. **I told her whiskey was my drink and I didn't need teacups and fine company to get it down. We parted friendly.**

Matt smiled at the thought of Althea Temple crossing words with Ben Pike. Althea had probably met more than her match in that exchange. He pondered more closely the final lines Ben had written:

Judge Vickers came to the mill yesterday,

which is the real reason for this letter. He was cagey. Said he had just stopped by. But he let drop he had been told Jordan and Wheat were scratching dirt and getting along all right. Seemed to interest him. The judge asked a lot of questions. I set him right about how you got the mill from Connally. He acted like he knew it already. My guess is, the bank won't be too unfriendly if you boys make a go of it this winter. Don't stop trying, anyhow. I'm too old to go back working for day wages, and too derned independent to live off my four boys if I go busted backing you.

Matt pondered that for days afterward. Who had told Judge Vickers that Jordan and Wheat were doing well? He wondered if Althea Temple had been pricked by conscience and had tried to make amends by influencing Judge Vickers in their favor. But when he tried to picture that midnight-haired young widow being influenced by her conscience, he ended up by snorting with disbelief. She had meddled for her own purposes and she'd keep on meddling without scruple until her will was satisfied.

The first freeze came out of the north on a sharp hard wind and high racing clouds. Of a sudden the world froze with bitter and crackling dry cold. Streams iced over in hours. At Camp One, where Matt was caught by the frigid gale, there was loud complaining from the tiered bunks about facing the icy blast outside.

But the men bolted huge platters of beans, salt meat and buckwheat cakes, and braved the biting dawn in thick Mackinaw coats, ear coverings, gloves, and woolen socks. It would be this way through the winter, often worse. Once started, the logging would not stop, save for Sunday lay-off.

The third afternoon following the freeze Matt was riding between Camp Three and Camp Two when he spotted a drift of greasy-white streamers above the pine tops, and caught the first dread smell of fire smoke. He wheeled his horse and galloped back toward Camp Three.

Camp Three was unaware. Matt's harsh order sent the chore boy firing gun signals. The camp blacksmith left his anvil, mounted a tote team horse he had been shoeing, and rode out into the woods to spread the alarm.

The camp foreman, a knotty Scotsman named MacLean, was the first in at a dead run. "Fire?" he panted. "It canna be at this time of year!"

"It's a long way off," Matt said. "And coming with the wind this way. Get your horses and ox teams ready to move. Take the rest of your men to the fire and try to hold it west of Clear Lake and that strip of marsh."

"There's ne'er been a pine fire stopped in a wind like this, laddie!" MacLean protested, shaking his head.

"You'll do what you can," Matt ordered. He swung into the saddle and spoke down to MacLean. "Try to keep pinching it to the west. Camp One and Two will come at it from the other side. If we can't pinch it in or hold it, we'll lose most of the timber we planned to cut this winter. There's no time to shift camps and cut new log roads."

MacLean was bellowing in rich Scotch brogue at approaching axe men as Matt rode away. Dubious as MacLean was, he was rock steady and dependable. He'd leave the logging area of Camp Three only when fire drove him out step by step.

Midway between Camp Three and Camp Two the smoke streamers were sifting thicker through the wind-laced

74

pine branches. Matt felt the cold clutch of disaster as he visualized distant flames feeding fiercely on the dry forest. Judging by the wind and smoke, a red swath of destruction was headed through the heart of their logging area.

He found Camp Two already alarmed. Warning had been sent to Camp One. An hour before dusk Matt led the vanguard of Camp Two out on the wooded shore of a mile-long narrow lake that had no name. North and east of the lake the fire was a wall of wind-whipped smoke and leaping geysers of flame.

Shorty Weaver, the foreman of Camp Two, wiped his rough Mackinaw sleeve across a sweaty face. "Look at the way them blazing hunks are blowin' on ahead!"

Matt looked up and studied the vast smoke billows swirling against the sky.

"The wind's dropping some, Shorty. There's a good chance of keeping the fire on the other side of the lake. Take all of your men up that way and start a fire strip from the end of the lake. I'll have Camp One start working a backfire line from this end of the lake."

"How're you going to backfire, the way the wind is?"

"I'm taking a chance on the wind dying out tonight."

"I guess anything's worth a try," Weaver muttered.

Sam Wheat arrived from Belleville three hours after dark. He stood on the lake's frozen shore with Matt. To the north and east of them the world was red with destruction. The hard wind had slackened and the blaze was advancing more slowly. Fire ran up the tall pines and spouted skyward in sheets of crimson. Spark clouds and embers whirled aloft on the updraft like gay and monstrous fireflies.

"I make it about six miles wide and spreading over toward Camp Three," Matt said.

"Our next year's cut," Sam said heavily. "And it's working into this year's cut. That fire never started natural."

"Tomorrow I'll see where it started and what I can find."

"If Bixby set it to stop us logging this winter, why didn't he fire it farther south?"

"A smart man would give room to spread. The wind was strong enough to bring it down on our camps anyway."

"Then good bye Jordan and Wheat."

"Exactly."

"I'll go with you in the morning," Sam said, hefting the axe he had brought. "You think there's a chance of back-firing?"

"Not much," Matt admitted. "We'll do what we can."

The swath left by the fire-line choppers looked hopelessly narrow among the tall trees. Men who had toiled all day worked on through the night. Lanterns cast miniature circles of ghostly pallor. The bite of hard-swung axes formed a never-ending tattoo. Hoarse cries of—"Timber! Timber!"—struck through the night with monotonous frequency, followed by the heavy crashing of falling trees.

Two miles southeast of the lake, across a small ridge, the fire line would strike the west bank of a narrow woods stream that meandered south and east toward Gopher Creek. Matt planned to backfire along that line if the wind dropped. The scant chance of keeping the fire north of the line had to be taken. Otherwise, Jordan and Wheat might as well pay off their men and hold the winter losses as small as possible.

Two hours after midnight the wind had almost died. Smoke formed a lazily drifting pall over the whole district. The fire was a sullen wall of flame moving slowly now.

Shorty Weaver sent men from the northern end of the lake. Matt held them at the foot of the lake while he studied the sky. He had just got a report that the fire line would be across the ridge and down to the streambank by daylight or a little later. The wind seemed to have died away completely. A vast umbrella of crimson-laced smoke hung against the sky.

"It's clouding up," one of the weary men commented.

Another jeered: "Can't tell smoke from clouds."

Matt turned to the man who had come from the advancing fire line. "I'm going to start the backfire here at the lake," he said. "Get about fifteen men back this way. We'll need them."

Water-soaked blanket squares were passed around. Ever after Matt was to remember the fateful silence as the first backfire flame was started among the fallen treetops north of the fire line. At first it was an uncertain, wavering, slowly spreading flame. Then, popping, crackling savagely, it climbed and spread.

Other backfires sparked out along the line. A tongue of flame roared up through high branches and exploded out of a pine top in an upsweep of sparks. Some of the sparks dropped on the fire line and across it, but they were small, dying as they fell.

A hungry wall of flame ate along the fire line and burned back north. Lanterns were not needed in the wild red glare through which men lunged with flailing blankets.

Dawn was a gray, cold, reluctant light through smoke, flame glow, and higher clouds. The backfire was sweeping along the fire line. Already smoldering trunks stood nakedly near the lake.

Sam came up with a black-smeared face. He was carrying a scorched blanket. "We going to make it, Matt?"

"No," Matt said. He looked up. "The wind's coming again."

Sam's grin was ghastly. "Did someone say we were lucky?"

The wind picked up almost imperceptibly. An hour later the first spot fire flared beyond the fire line and leaped out of control.

Matt sent an order down the line for all men to get back to the lake. They'd done what they could. Strength was not left for a new fire line this day.

Shorty Weaver's men joined them. They watched the east, where the old fire front and the new were spreading in mounting fury.

"She'll get everything this time," one bearded chopper said heavily.

Men looked without much interest when a shout came from a towering Norwegian standing at the lake edge. The man was gesturing overhead.

"She's come, by golly! Bane snow! Snow!"

A moment later Sam thrust out his arm before Matt. "Look," he said, his voice shaking.

Together they stared in silent fascination at one tiny flake of snow resting delicately on Sam's rough Mackinaw sleeve.

IX

Snow! In hesitant flakes at first, then in bolder swirls, the snow fell on flames and unburned pine. It came faster, heavier, as the long-dry skies opened.

Matt ordered the men back to the camps. Flames still leaped and devoured. But the wind was slackening again, the snowflakes turning large and wet. Pine branches and tindery needles on the ground were being covered by a white protecting mantle. Nothing would be gained by remaining to watch the dying blaze.

The snow was inches deep, falling thicker, faster, when Matt rode into Belleville. He was desperately tired. Elation over the snowstorm was tempered by the thought of how close to disaster he and Sam had come. Not only themselves, but Ben Pike, who had gambled so recklessly on them.

Delaying only to leave his horse at the livery barn, Matt went up to his hotel room and dropped off in sodden sleep. He felt better when he rolled out after dark.

A glance out the window showed night in the roiling grip of a mild blizzard. Matt smiled with satisfaction, washed in the tin basin of cold water, and went downstairs for dinner.

More people than usual were down there in the hard chairs by the roaring fireplace. The storm had driven everyone indoors. The tumult and music beyond the partition were louder than Matt had heard since the previous winter. He stepped through the narrow doorway into stale waves of stove heat and whiskey stench, rank tobacco smoke and the heady perfume of Big Lena's dancing girls.

This was almost like pay day. Heavy-booted lumberjacks waltzed girls recklessly on the dance floor. The bar was lined deeply. Poker tables at the back were crowded. Men who recognized Matt were eager to hear the final word about the timber fire. They crowded around him while he had the drink he wanted before eating.

"It was a close shave," Matt told them.

Gates, a small-time timber man from farther down the Waymego, observed: "Funny how a fire would start way back in there this time of year."

79

An awkward silence fell.

Matt finished his drink. "A fire can start in a lot of ways," he told Gates.

He left them restless with questions that no man wanted to voice.

Big Lena was in his path before he got to the door. In stiff white silk, with lace across her full bosom and shoulders, glinting rings and gleaming bracelets, hair piled in a distinguished roll, she had never appeared so stately.

"You look unusually well tonight, ma'am," Matt assured her.

Big Lena flushed under her powder. For a moment her eyes held a lonely hurt.

"The things I see in my mirror never look well, Matt Jordan. Will you buy me that drink now?"

"It'll be a privilege, ma'am."

Matt was holding her chair politely at a table by the wall when Bart Bixby stepped in from the hotel side and saw him. Bixby was shaved and dressed in his St. Louis clothes. His eyebrows went up in faint amusement. Tige Ellis followed through the narrow doorway with Mackinaw open and snow still melting on his shoes and shoulders.

Bixby ignored his companion. He was smiling easily as he came to the table where Matt had seated himself.

"Your pardon for interrupting," he apologized with easy courtesy. "I came in on the Indian Town stage just before dark and heard you'd had a bad woods fire."

"I can see it was a big surprise," Matt said mildly.

"Naturally. Do you need any help?"

"It's out. Not much damage done. Our winter's timber is still there."

"I'm glad to hear it. Call on me anytime." Bixby looked at Big Lena. "No wonder you're celebrating with the local

80

. . . er . . . ladies." Bixby seemed amused as he joined Tige Ellis at the bar.

"At least," said Big Lena roughly, "he leaves my girls alone. More's the pity."

"How's that, ma'am?"

"They're used to hurt," Big Lena said, shrugging. "They've lost the things most women dream about. He'll take some sweet girl who knows no better and he'll break her heart as callously as he'd whip a horse."

Bottles of St. Louis ale were put on the table between them. When the waiter left, Big Lena set her bottle and glass aside. "One of my girls had a visitor last night . . . a little logger named Byers. He was drunk and he's been drunk all day."

"I don't know him."

"It isn't pay day, but he had money," Big Lena said. "When he heard about the timber fire last night, he was drunk enough to laugh and say, if the fire didn't stop Jordan and Wheat, something else would."

Matt poured the cold ale slowly. "Evidently this Byers doesn't like us."

"Why should he?" asked Big Lena. "He works for Bixby and Smith."

Matt sampled the ale before he glanced at the bar. Bart Bixby was standing there alone, back to them.

"Where could I find this Byers, ma'am?"

"That's what I thought you'd want to know, Matt Jordan. He got too drunk. They dragged him in the back room to sleep it off."

"Does Bixby know he's there?"

Lena shrugged. Worry darkened her look. "You won't talk about this, Matt? Hennessy's not bad to work for. But he'd not stand us girls taking sides."

"I'll bear it in mind," Matt promised. He stood up, leaving the ale glass full. "How will I be sure I'm talking to Byers?"

"He's wearing Chippewa moccasins."

Bart Bixby was still at the bar when Matt walked back past the crowded dance floor and the poker tables. Several narrow storerooms opened off a rough-floored center passage. There was a back door. The cold back room was dark. Someone snored heavily.

Matt struck a match. Two men were sprawled on the floor. They had on lumberjack boots, not moccasins. Fresh bits of snow had been tracked in.

Matt turned back into the passage and opened the rear door. Wind and snow swirled in his face. Snow lay inches deep on the steps outside. Light from a second-story window dropped feeble radiance on footprints that had entered the building and gone out again. The departing prints looked as if a heavy burden had made the man lurch off balance.

The wind had driving force. Next door, the log stage station was dark. The building beyond was dark. The faint aura of light vanished back in the storm. Matt could barely see the tracks he followed.

He passed the stage station and adjoining building and turned with the tracks toward the street. He almost failed to see the dark figure that had been waiting around the building corner. The storm was in his ears and eyes. But he did see the vicious tongue of flame from a gun muzzle. Then he fell.

Matt heard the muted wind. He sensed the sleepy seep of cold into muscle and bone. The slow steady beat of pain in his chest stirred memory. He sat up, breaking through drifted snow. Death could not be like this, all storm, snow, darkness.

He staggered up. Heavy cap and earflaps had protected his head. A bullet had slashed his coat. With stiff fingers Matt explored the shirt pocket over his heart. Twisted bits of metal and fragments of glass in the pocket had been his repeater watch. The bullet, Matt realized dully, had driven the watchcase against his chest and had glanced off. Matt laughed. The harsh sound whipped away on the wind. The thick snow was a blinding swirl about him as he beat stiff arms against his body.

The tracks he had been following were lost now under the driving, drifting, white blanket. Moving awkwardly and with effort, Matt waded to the plank walk. The stage station door was unlocked. The dark room inside had fire chunks still glowing in the wood stove.

Matt piled on more wood. He stamped about the room, rubbing his hands and beating at his arms and legs, and after a while the numb lethargy of cold retreated. His chest was badly bruised where the watchcase had driven against it. Otherwise, he seemed all right when he left the stage station and pushed through the front entrance of the barroom.

Bart Bixby was not in the long, crowded room. Matt caught Big Lena's questioning look through the haze of tobacco smoke. He shook his head slightly and walked into the hotel half of the building.

Bart Bixby was among those who sat and stood about the fireplace. He was pulling on a half-smoked cigar, his back to the fire. He gave Matt a startled look. Ash fell from the cigar as he bit hard on the end. Then, with an easy smile, Bixby moved away from the fire.

"Still celebrating?" he asked. His eyes had no friendliness; they looked muddy and uncertain.

Matt was aware of heads turning. He wanted it that way, with witnesses. "Bixby," he said, "I've come to know you pretty well. I don't think you've troubled to know me."

"I suppose you know what you're driving at, Jordan. Is something wrong?"

"Something's been wrong. I'll set you right about it. Don't ever forget it. I won't."

Bart Bixby's strained smile was shading to a sneer when Matt hit him.

He knew as he struck that Bart Bixby had been deluded by many things, chief of which was that magnificent self-confidence of his. The blow exploded on Bixby's jaw with an impact that reached all through the room. Bixby went down with a surprised look on his face.

"He's had his warning now," Matt said. "The rest is up to him."

Matt started to the stairway, and then stopped as he saw Althea Temple and Matha Vickers halfway down, frozen by the violence they had witnessed.

Althea Temple recovered first and ran lightly down the stairs.

"He's hurt," she said huskily to Matt.

"And wiser, I hope, ma'am," Matt told her coldly. "Are you satisfied with what your meddling's done?"

She went to Bart Bixby without reply. Matt hesitated and mounted the creaking steps to Matha, who had not moved.

"I saw it," Matha said in a low voice. "How cowardly!"

"Our ideas of cowardice probably differ, ma'am. Are you girls here in Belleville alone?"

"My uncle is talking with Kirby Smith. He wanted information about the logging camps for his bank, and planned to take us on to Milwaukee and Chicago. We'll leave as soon as sleighs can travel over the stage road."

"You shouldn't have come." Matt's smile was ironical. "Dog eat dog isn't pleasant to watch, ma'am. If I've hurt you by hurting Bixby, it was not my intention."

"You seem to have hurt Althea more," Matha said coolly.

Matt turned, looking down. Althea Temple, in her fine dress, was kneeling on the damp and dirty floor, one arm supporting Bart Bixby's lolling head. She was wiping his slack face with a lace-edged handkerchief. Matt thought she had never been so beautiful as now, with compassion glowing on her face.

"She looks as if she loves him," Matt muttered in amazement.

"So? You've been blinder than I thought, Mister Jordan. But not so blind, I hope, as to think this is the last you'll hear from Bart Bixby. Will you let me pass? Althea should not be down there alone."

Matt stepped aside, remembering too late the rough woods cap still on his head. He snatched it off and watched her leave him, blonde, slender, graceful.

In his room, Matt took a revolver and gun belt from his carpetbag. He locked the door, propped the single chair solidly under the knob, and went to sleep.

At daybreak Matt floundered through the drifts to the office to pick up a pair of snowshoes and a rifle. He left a brief note for Ike Bowman, and started back to Camp One through the dying blizzard.

Sam Wheat received the news with grim satisfaction.

"I guess this means everybody packs a gun from now on," he said.

"It does."

They were seated at one of the tables in the big log building. The camp crew was breaking out roads. The cook had set out beans, fried meat, coffee, buckwheat cakes, and a pitcher of molasses. Sam leaned his elbows on the table, his freckled, weather-beaten face hard. "You think that fellow Byers fired our timber?"

"Looks that way," Matt said, stirring more sugar in his coffee. "Bixby must have suspected Byers was dangerous drunk and sent Tige Ellis around back of the dance hall to get Byers out of the way."

"Bixby don't overlook any bets. What do you think he'll do now?"

"I don't know. We'll be ready for trouble, though. I want the men to go armed and stay out of Belleville. Our log cut is the only thing that will pull us through. It's got to be big."

"Watch the tallies climb from now on," Sam promised.

Sam was a prophet. They had hired good men at high wages and they fed them well. Week by week the log tallies mounted in record-breaking jumps.

The threat of danger seemed to help. To a man, almost, the crews went armed and watchful. The story of Bart Bixby's tumble in Hennessy's Tavern went through all three camps, embellished by retelling.

In January there was a freak thaw for two days, and then another blizzard. The regular snows were heavy.

Reports said the Bixby and Smith camps were logging hard. They seemed to have no time for making trouble. Kirby Smith had gone to St. Louis for the winter. By mid-February Matt had seen Bart Bixby only twice in Belleville. Each time Bixby passed with a stony face.

Big Lena told Matt that Byers had not reappeared at Hennessy's Tavern. "They must have killed him," she said matter-of-factly. She was at the bar again beside Matt. Her lowered voice was troubled. "I don't like the way that Tige Ellis smiles at me when he's drinking. He knows something and there's no good in it."

"You've nothing to worry about, Lena," Matt said.

"No worries or regrets," said Lena pensively. "I have nothing to lose. Don't get careless. Bixby will never forget you."

"That suits me."

"His eyes have got frozen hell in them, Matt. It's there every time he comes in."

Smiling, Matt asked: "What about my eyes?"

"Worried," Big Lena said calmly. "And not all over Bart Bixby, either. You're lonely, Matt." Lena's face softened. "I hear everything. She was pretty on the stairs that night, wasn't she?"

Matt felt his face flush. "You're speaking of Bixby's friend, ma'am."

"When the road was open, I saw her leave. Bixby handed her into the sleigh and tucked the buffalo robes about her and her friend. She hardly saw him. She was looking around for someone not there."

"Nonsense, Lena."

Big Lena shrugged. "Take care of yourself until the ice breaks and you go with the rafts to Saint Louis. I can feel trouble in the air. It won't wait forever."

Days later Sam said the same thing. They were below the dam on Gopher Creek. A great rollway of carefully piled logs towered on the bank, waiting for that spring day when they would crash and thunder into flood water rushing toward the Waymego and the great raft booms at Indian Slough in the Mississippi.

"They're still not in Saint Louis," Sam said, estimating

the mountain of logs. "What happens if Bixby and Smith drive the Waymego ahead of us?"

"I'd like to know," Matt admitted.

Winter lasted through March, frigid, blustery. The yoked ox teams steadily plodded the tote roads. The ring of axes, the rhythmic whip of saws, and crash of falling timber echoed in the deep woods from dawn to dark. But spring was in the longer days, the brighter sun, the slackening bite of the wind.

Preparations were rushed for the log drive and the raft building in Indian Slough. Men turned out in the early dawn laughing and rough-housing as if the sap of spring were fast rising in their winter-hardened bodies. Then, abruptly, in a day and night, the south wind came, hard and warm.

The first bare patches on the south slopes widened with amazing speed. Life began to mutter and surge under the stream ice. 10,000 tiny rivulets crawled off the earth and joined the midday melt. The sun rose warm again, and, before it set, the break-up had begun and the ice was running.

X

Matt stood in the slush and mud of Gopher Creek's bank and watched the open sluice gates in the dam upstream. The rush of imprisoned water was a deep, low-toned growl laced by the sharper sounds of breaking ice.

Down the bank Long John, in calk-soled boots, stepped carefully in the slippery mud at the base of the rollway. Long John carried a peavy and seemed oblivious to the mass of piled logs on the bank above him. Shoulders hunched, he stalked the key log of that vast pile of sixteen-foot timber. Men posted up and down the bank watched intently with Matt. They studied the rise of frothing water, thick with clashing ice chunks.

Long John ignored the water as he stabbed with the peavy point, hooked into the key log, and threw his weight against the stout handle.

The key log showed no movement. No audible sound reached through the roar of water and ice plunging past the open dam. But a straining animation seemed to run through the vast mass of inert timber, like a monster bracing itself to plunge. Long John heaved and swung on the peavy handle. Then, of a sudden, he jerked the peavy free and wheeled back, his calk shoes digging, hard and deep, as he ran for the safety of the unobstructed bank.

Slow, imperceptible movement flowed through the rollway mass as he ran. Timber groaned and cracked. Then, with drawn-out thunder, the high-stacked logs pitched down toward the foamy current. Long John, barely safe from destruction, shook his peavy and laughed up at Matt before he turned to watch the first water-borne logs surge toward the Waymego and the Mississippi rafting booms.

Other rollways along Gopher Creek had their turn at emptying into the rising flood. Along the banks calk-shoed men with peavies and pick poles watchfully nursed the floating logs. Now and then they had to leap on floating timber, stamping calks deep, balancing with easy skill as they pulled or shoved. Only men who had seen the swift interlocking of a log jam could know the need for vigilance along every rod of stream.

That same day Matt got word that the Waymego was carrying Bixby and Smith logs. He rode to the mouth of

Gopher Creek, where new thickets were growing in the old slash. Surging logs were coming downstream. The first logs of Gopher Creek were nosing out among them. Occasionally they blocked in masses at the Gopher's mouth. Jordan and Wheat men posted there fought with pick poles to keep the grinding logs away from the bank.

"Any Bixby and Smith men been along here?" Matt asked a big Irishman who had just leaped back to the bank from a floating log.

"Faith, no!" he was answered. " 'Tis a dirty welcome they'll get if they come through our drive."

"You'll start no trouble unless it's brought to you," Matt warned.

But he had the tense, suppressed sensation of waiting. Sam Wheat had taken his picked gang of raft builders down to the sorting booms at Indian Slough. The logs were branded on the ends and would be sorted. It was too easy. Bart Bixby was not the man to have it so.

There was a trail through the slash to an old logging road by which a man could reach Camp One. Matt was riding deep in the slash when he heard a shot behind. He reined in his horse and listened. He heard the distant hail of his name, and he answered.

A hard-ridden horse burst into view on the brush trail, with Long John in the saddle. "Trouble, Matt!" he said. "One of our men is at Camp One with a bullet through him! Bixby and Smith have took the riverbank at Little Devil Rapids. We had three men there. Only this one got away!" Long John spat into the snow slop. "I figgered you'd want me along."

"Come on!" Matt said.

There was still sunlight when they reached the clearing at Camp One. Bill Irwin, the gray-haired foreman, was outside the log building with a dozen of his brawniest woodsmen.

"It's that yellow-haired young fellow named Svenson," Irwin said. He gestured with a gnarled hand. "I brought these men in. Thought you might want 'em quick. Svenson's inside."

Svenson lay on a blanket in a lower bunk. A bloody bandage covered his shoulder. He could still smile. "I t'ink plenty trouble," he told Matt. "Wilson got busted head. That Fred Rapp got gun stuck in his back."

"What do they want, Svenson?"

"Yus' trouble, I t'ink."

"It don't make sense," Long John said. "If they just want their drive to go through, they needn't jump our men."

Bill Irwin was a gnarled, rugged state of Maine man who had seen better than thirty log drives in as many seasons. "Suppose they don't want the drive to go through?" he asked gruffly. "I seen it happen on Rapid River when I was a youngster. Had a timber feud. Old Jed McLarney took charge of White Rapids with a bunch of French-Canadians an' started a log jam that tied up the river all that season. They used up half the blastin' powder in Maine before they got the mess cleared out.

Long John swore. "I wouldn't have thought of that! But nothin' sings better than an old tune. What do you think, Matt?"

Frowning, Matt said: "Irwin, have you got any blasting powder left?"

"Nary a grain."

"We may not need it. Tell your men to bring pick poles and peavies along with the guns. We'll short cut to the Rapids by Coon Ridge tote road and that slash beyond the ridge. Better ride the tote teams or we'll get there after dark."

High clouds were shot with crimson from the vanishing sun when they tied the horses in brush and old slash half a mile from Little Devil Rapids.

"You know what you're up against," Matt told the others. "Hard to tell how many men we'll find or what they'll do. There's still a chance to go back."

They looked at him indulgently, not deeming the warning worth answering. Bill Irwin spoke for them mildly. "Nobody come this far to go back."

Matt led them forward. As they neared the rapids, the even monotone of water past the rocks was strangely muted, tortured by harsher overtones. Matt sorted out the dull grind of timber, discordant undertones of strain. He looked at Irwin.

Irwin nodded. "Big jam," he said briefly. "What'd I tell you?"

The sharp snap of a rifle report cut off Matt's answer.

"Spread out," Matt ordered over his shoulder. "Shoot at anything you see moving. They've made the rules."

Of a sudden he was alone, hard put to guess where his men, all skillful woodsmen, were advancing. Off to right and left a second and a third shot had answered the first. After that, silence held. Rifle cocked, Matt advanced with easy, quiet, and restlessly probing eyes. He reached the riverbank without being challenged.

He stopped in the overgrown logging path and looked about warily. If the signs could be believed, the men they stalked had retreated after the three shots.

Matt parted the fringe of bushes and stepped out on the riverbank. For some moments he stood motionlessly, taking in the tangle of big logs from bank to bank. Little Devil

Rapids was a full mile long, running, fast and tortured, past
big rocks. Logs had piled on logs, upended, driven in at
treacherous angles. And still the mass of floating timber
continued to pile and interlock, higher, farther back from
the jam. Streams of water shot through the logs, swirled
under them, but the main river was still backing upstream.

A shout off to the right told that the two Jordan and
Wheat men had been found. Still no other shots had been
fired. Matt called the men in. Rapp, a short-bearded logger,
was rubbing rope marks on his wrists and swearing.

"They come on us before we knowed what was up," he
said bitterly. "Svenson run an' they shot at him. That Tige
Ellis told us to be quiet or we'd get pitched into the river."

"What did they want?" Matt asked.

"Nobody said. We couldn't see the river. Sounded like
they was working down the bank and out on the river rocks.
They seemed mighty pleased when the log jam started."

It's a whopper," Long John said. He shook his head.
"Hard to believe Bixby would cut his own throat like this to
get back at another man. If this jam ain't busted quick,
there's no telling how long the river stays locked."

"Bixby could ruin us and still log next winter," Matt
said. He looked at Irwin. "What do you think about it,
Bill?"

Irwin had gnawed deeply on a dry twist of tobacco. He
champed a moment, filling his cheek, and then laid his gun
on the ground. He took a peavy from the nearest logger and
started down the bank. Matt and Long John followed suit.

The river rocks were dark and exposed in the shallow
stream below the jam. Jumping from one slick rock to the
next, wading knee deep at times, Bill Irwin led them out.
The face of the jam towered above them in an irregular
wall of interlocked logs that quivered and strained under

the mighty pressure behind.

Matt lifted his voice. "Most of these logs are ours!"

Long John swept his glance over the branded log butts, shrugged, and continued his prowling along the base of the jam, looking for the key log of the jam.

A third of the way out, where the current raced between two rocky protuberances, Bill Irwin paused. He stabbed his peavy point into a base log, blocked fully at one end and canted up against a sloping rock at the other. He tested the log with his peavy and spat into the water.

"Work this one an' a couple more loose an' she might move."

"I believe you're right, Bill," said Matt. "But this is no place for you. Get to shore."

"There ain't nothin' wrong with me, Matt Jordan!"

"Get to shore!" Matt repeated. "We haven't got much time before dark."

Irwin started heavily back to shore.

"Well, John," Matt said. "You know what we're up against if this thing breaks loose."

Long John laughed and hooked his peavy into the log. Thereafter they worked in silence, two lone figures attacking one log in the shallow riverbed.

They were panting and sweating as they finally succeeded in working the higher end of the log almost imperceptibly up the rock slope that blocked it.

Abruptly the log slid over the rock. For one breathless instant they poised to run, then relaxed as nothing happened.

Matt stabbed his peavy into a second log. "Maybe this one," he said.

They took out three logs. The purple shadows were pressing about them as they started working on a fourth.

"Damned if we won't have to clear it out stick by stick if this keeps up!" Long John blurted, breathing hard.

Matt grinned and shifted his peavy for a fresh attack. Of a sudden, he stood motionlessly, his grip tight on the peavy, his head cocked to listen, eyes watchful along the face of the jam.

The log to which he was hooked transmitted the barest shudder up the peavy handle. There was a *crack* like a pistol report, then a slow, deep, and terrible murmur of movement. The log snagged to his peavy began to move at one end under the thrust of timber behind it.

Matt dropped the peavy. "She's coming! Get out of here!"

The beginning seemed slow and deliberate. What followed came upon them with awful speed.

Logs thrust out of the jam just back of Long John's retreat. The face of the jam began to bulge. Between Matt and the shore a tangle of timber began to thrust out. There was no time to shout to Long John. Matt leaped to the groaning front of the jam, using hands and steel calks to get up on top of the mass. He threw one look back and saw Long John following. He gained the top, caught balance as a log shifted under him, and saw Long John at his heels. Then, with a series of tremendous reports, the world went mad and the jam broke in leaping logs, surging water. Suddenly there was no footing, only plunging logs, tossing water, and the vague blur of men running on the bank as the jam underfoot hurtled downstream.

Each wild leap from log to log seemed the last. A desperate will to survive kept muscles moving. With a sort of dazed surprise, Matt suddenly realized one great leap had put him knee deep in water, with one foot on the muddy bank. He fought his way to solid ground.

He was gasping, shaking, when he looked back for Long

John. There was no sign of him in that wild mêlée of white water and plunging timber.

Old Bill Irwin, despite his age, was one of the first men to reach Matt.

"A log turned under him and he fell in," Irwin panted. "Ain't no use lookin' for him."

"Leave part of your men to keep the jam cleared. We'll patrol the bank down toward Big Devil Rapids," Matt said in a tight voice.

Four men were with him and night was fully about them when they reached the rush of Big Devil Rapids. They had not found Long John's body.

XI

Belleville was only a mile away. Matt walked into town alone. He was stony-faced as he headed for the Bixby and Smith office.

The place was dark. He turned back to the small slab office of Jordan and Wheat. When he stepped in, Ike Bowman, the bookkeeper, turned to him with relief.

"I'm glad they found you," Bowman said. "It seemed important."

"What seemed important?" Matt asked.

"I thought the man found you and told you, Mister Jordan. Big Lena wants you. She says she's got to see you. Oh, yes, here's a letter that's been here two days."

The letter was from Ben Pike. The harsh lines washed from Matt's face as he read:

All we need now is logs. If you and Sam get

the winter cut down here, we'll be in the clear. I've got reasons for thinking so. Judge Vickers was by again. The judge said he missed you in Belleville just after freeze-up. But he said you seemed to be set for a big winter in the woods. I can't make out the old turkey. He seems interested in you, for some reason, although he admits he never talked with you. But he's got a reputation as a square shooter. I think if you boys come out of the winter all right, you'll find the welcome mat at the bank dusted off.

Matt put the letter in his pocket. "Is Bart Bixby around town?"

"He was two days ago. That's the last I've seen of him, sir."

"Long John is dead," Matt said heavily. "We're going to miss him, Bowman."

He walked out, a great weariness filling him. Some of it was weariness of the heart at losing a man like Long John. Money could be made. But loyalty had to be found and cherished.

He guessed, as he stepped into Hennessy's Tavern, that Big Lena had been watching the door and waiting for him. She met him before he reached the bar.

"Go to that little log house of mine back of the livery stable," she said under her breath. "I'll get there before you and unlock the door."

Matt ordered whiskey at the bar. He hardly felt its bite. The deep and growing glow of anger within him needed no whiskey warmth.

Big Lena had thrown a shawl over her shoulders and slipped out the back way. Matt went out the front and around to the cabin behind the livery barn. Heavy curtains barely showed the light within as Matt knocked on the thick plank door. Big Lena opened it.

Matt blinked a moment at the home-like atmosphere of hand-made curtains, rag rugs, pictures on the walls, St. Louis furniture, and the cheerful fireplace. There was a rocking chair before the fireplace and a sewing basket on the floor beside it.

"Here's the only man in Belleville besides you who makes me feel I'm a lady," Big Lena said. "I asked him to find out about Byers. He found out . . . and got shot."

The man lay blanketed on Big Lena's narrow bed in the corner. He was a logger with ear-long black hair and an untrimmed beard.

"He's been logging for Bixby and Smith. Name is Starkey," Lena added.

"You don't know me, suh?" the man asked, smiling a little.

"Good God!" Matt exclaimed as the voice struck memory. "Tom Connally! You're supposed to be dead."

"My lives seem numerous, suh."

"This," said Big Lena weakly, "flabbergasts me."

"And me," Matt admitted. He sat on the bed. "Why didn't you come to me sooner, Connally?"

"A gambler named Kram put me off the upper deck of the *Silver Eagle*," Connally said. "A man thinks fast when he finds himself drowning. Kram knew our mutual friend Bixby. Kram had suggested a poker game before I played with you, suh. He seemed sure my Bank City mill was burning before we sighted it from the river. My business affairs had become complicated since I started doing business with Bixby and his friends. It occurred to me that being a gentleman was not profitable. I walked north to Bixby's logging camps and hired out as Starkey. I had no trouble keeping out of Bixby's way."

"What about Byers?"

"He came to Bixby's Camp Five. A quart of whiskey made him talkative and he admitted he had set fire to your timber . . . also my Bank City mill last fall. Ellis paid him, with Bixby money."

Tom Connally stirred weakly under the blanket. "Byers was to help Ellis start a log jam after a few Bixby and Smith logs were sent downstream."

Matt nodded, his face hardening as he thought of Long John.

"The main Bixby and Smith cut is to wait on rollways until your drive is out of the way." Connally smiled. "Ellis found me questioning Byers and called me a spy. It was a pleasure to hit him, suh. But other men shot at me. I almost didn't get away."

Matt sat intently. "The log jam and Bixby holding back his logs doesn't make sense. I wish I had Byers."

"I believe, suh, he was going to join Bixby at Indian Slough."

"I think I'll ride to Indian Slough," Matt decided. He stood up. "Connally, you're in the sawmill business with Sam and me."

Indian Slough, six miles long, was wide and sluggish below the Waymego mouth. Here, in chain-linked booms, the floating timber was held. Great auger holes were bored in the raft logs. End to end and side-by-side, the logs were bound into stringers by bracing birch limbs held with split burr oak loops that were pegged into the auger holes. The long stringers, each with a large plank sweep at the end, would be bound into rafts, and the huge rafts would go down the Mississippi to the sawmills.

The sun blazed overhead as Matt turned from the road into a little used trail and came to the lower end of Indian Slough before turning upstream to the booms. He had ridden all night.

He advanced with quiet watchfulness, rifle ready across the saddle. The raft builders stayed in slab shanties among oak and sycamore trees at the north end of the slough. On a day like this, men should be busy splitting burr oak, over-hauling boats, watching the Waymego mouth for the van-guard of the log drive.

A quarter mile from the Jordan and Wheat camp Matt tied the horse and went forward on foot, wondering about the unusual silence ahead.

He sighted a faint drift of smoke from the roof hole of his camp, but when he reached the doorway, the place was empty. A logger's cap lay on the floor inside. Coals in the fireplace were dying. There was no preparation for the midday meal.

The new camp for the Bixby and Smith men was in a clearing farther up the slough bank. Matt circled back through the timber and brush, crossing the narrow Indian Slough wagon road, and came to the Bixby and Smith clearing from the land side. The new slab building on the bank faced south. Matt approached silently from the east side, where there was no window. He heard angry swearing inside, and recognized the voice of Sam Wheat demanding water.

Someone said impatiently: "Bring the water bucket in, Joe, and let's get on with this card game. They'll have us workin' soon enough."

"They'll have you hung soon enough, too," Sam said viciously.

Matt cocked the heavy Sharps rifle. He was soundless in

the soft footing as he stepped around the shanty wall. Water bucket and tin dipper sat on a wooden box in front of him.

A man stepped out through the cabin door, blinking in the sunlight. He was at the bucket before he saw the waist-high rifle muzzle. He stopped, his burly shoulders hunched, hands halted in the first gesture toward his revolver holster. He was Joe Pick, who had stopped the Madison stage and followed Sam.

"You goin' to stay with that water all day?" the impatient voice called.

Matt gestured with the gun muzzle. Pick read the order rightly, lifted the water bucket, and turned stiffly back through the low doorway. Matt crowded at his heels into the dim light inside, and stepped left and put his back against the rough slab wall.

"Water for everyone," Matt said. "Who reaches first?"

Two of them faced him across the board eating table. Rifles leaned against the wall behind them. Sitting backed to the walls, arms and legs roped securely, were Sam Wheat and his men. Sam gave a whoop and said: "Now we start to laugh!"

The table overturned with a *crash*. Matt marked the bearded logger who had heaved the table over and dropped behind it, whirling for one of the rifles. Matt fired through the table top.

Pick dropped the water bucket and lunged for the doorway. Matt hurled the rifle between his legs, tripping him and sending him in a reeling plunge through the doorway.

Beyond the overturned table a second man was snapping a revolver. The report sounded louder than the Sharps rifle. When the man saw he had missed, he hurled his gun and dropped frantically behind the overturned table, yelling: "I give up!"

101

From where Sam was sitting he could see out through the doorway, and he called out: "That fellow kept going outside! You got the first one behind the table. Cut us loose and get your other men ready before Bixby comes with his bunch."

"You!" Matt ordered the man who had surrendered. "Get up and cut them loose." While the fellow was slashing the ropes, Matt picked up his rifle and asked Sam what had happened.

"They got us after daylight this morning," Sam said ruefully. "Brought us over here. Bixby and the rest of them are watching the road to see that no one comes. Funny you didn't meet any of them."

"I came along the slough bank. What's Bixby got on his mind?" Matt was reloading the rifle.

Sam rubbed his freed wrist and stretched stiffened muscles. "They're waiting for the log drive to come down. Bixby says it's due to come with a rush. He promised you'd be too busy around Belleville to send many men down this way at first."

"We had a log jam. Bixby was almost right," Matt said. "He started trouble at the rapids for a blind. He's holding his own logs back and our drive is coming down solid in the Waymego. There won't be any of our men here to catch it and it'll scatter down the Mississippi for five hundred miles."

Sam's square jaw ridged hard. "They put our guns there in that top bunk. How many men did you bring?"

"Only twenty-three. They're on the bank below our camp."

"Eight of us here . . . and you makes thirty-two. Bixby's got fourteen now, counting that skunk who got away. Matt, I guess we can hold the Waymego mouth until we put the last raft out on the river."

"I mean to. Long John got killed in the log jam Bixby ordered started. There's a score to settle over that. Let's get back to the rest of the men and hunt Bixby and his bunch."

"What about this one?"

"Keep his guns and let him go."

Sam grumbled at that, and then jumped as a rifle shot across the clearing drove a bullet through the open door.

"That will bring our men," Matt commented, almost pleased. "We'll run this one out and duck down the bank and hold them off." Matt swung the rifle muzzle on the prisoner. "Go out running."

"They'll shoot afore they see who I am!"

"It's your chance. Ready, boys?"

Their bearded prisoner took a gulping breath and dashed outside, bawling a warning not to shoot.

They plunged after him, guns firing across the clearing. Answering shots failed to stop any of them as they bolted under the tall sycamores on the slough bank and gained the shelter of the slope.

Matt turned right toward the Waymego mouth. The others followed him through the gaunt thickets until the clearing was well behind.

"Aren't you getting pretty far away from the rest of our men?" Sam panted.

Matt listened for a moment. He said: "I rode from Belleville alone, boys."

Sam's eyes bulged. "We ain't got any help?"

"Twenty-three men that Bixby's bunch will be seeing behind every bush, Sam. That's why I let that fellow go. It's up to you men to split up and act like thirty of our men dodging through these woods. Can you do it?"

They were rough and powerful men, the pick of the loggers and rafting crews. Obie White, a hand taller than six feet, showed his teeth in a grin that spoke for the others. "If we can't lick 'em, we can worry 'em," he said. "Come on, boys . . . scatter out an' go Injun on 'em."

"I like a gamble," Sam said, inspecting his big-barreled Colt revolver. "But if our bluff is called in this one, Matt, Bixby takes everything, don't he?" Sam shook his head. "What are you goin' to do?"

"Try to think like Bart Bixby will be thinking," Matt answered.

For some minutes after Sam left, Matt squatted motionlessly in thought. Then, with loose and quiet strides, he worked through the trees to the upper end of Indian Slough. Several times he stopped as gunfire sounded in the distance behind him. None of it settled into steady firing.

Matt stopped in a thicket and looked out at the Waymego mouth below him. The main log boom was anchored to the bank with a heavy chain. Any hour now the Waymego would bring the logs down. But more than logs would come down against that heavy boom. The past and the future would come, too, on the spring freshet—the years ahead for Sam Wheat, Ben Pike, Matt Jordan. Matt stood thinking of Long John. And then, queerly enough, of Matha Vickers. Running footsteps brought him alert.

The heavily panting man who ran down the bank path some yards away did not see him. Matt watched him put his rifle on the ground, pick up a light sledge, and step toward the shackle of the massive boom chain. Matt stepped out into the open and cocked the rifle.

"Not this year, Bixby," he said.

Bart Bixby whirled around. His flannel shirt was open at the neck. He had not shaved for a day. He was as rough-looking as one of his loggers, and he stood in tense and furious anger.

Matt moved carefully down the bank. "I thought you'd try this, Bixby."

Matt's foot slipped on the soft bank. He had changed from calk shoes to make the saddle ride from Belleville. As he slid off balance, Bart Bixby dropped the sledge and dived for his rifle.

Matt had one chance to shoot as he regained balance. He thought of Matha Vickers saying: *How cowardly!* With an oath he dropped the rifle and covered the rest of the distance in one leaping plunge.

His full weight struck Bixby as the man was straightening with the cocked rifle. The gun went off harmlessly to one side as they sprawled together, rolling on the muddy ground.

Bixby was hard-muscled and fast. He came lunging up, clutching at the revolver in Matt's holster. Matt caught the wrist with both his hands. A bone-breaking twist made Bixby drop the revolver. They stamped it in the soft wet earth as they came to their feet. Bixby's fist struck Matt in the mouth. Matt slipped again as he jumped back and spat blood.

The soft, weed-grown footing was some twenty feet wide, with only a slight slope into the water. Wet earth clung to their shoes as they stepped around each other. Matt spat blood again, calm as he studied the blaze in Bixby's eyes.

Bixby rushed him. Matt met him solidly, coldly driving blows that found Bixby's face, stopped him, straightened him up, drove him, reeling, with a split lip and a mashed nose.

Matt followed him as he had followed Tige Ellis on the

steamboat. Bixby beat at him. Matt took the blows and walked in, smashing in one unending fury of driving fists. They wore each other down fast.

Matt could almost sense the moment when Bart Bixby weakened. He smiled then with a bloody and swelling mouth.

Bart Bixby's eyes grew haunted as he saw the smile. He stepped back. Matt knocked a fist aside and struck Bixby in the face twice with terrible force. Bixby's eyes were glazing as the third blow struck his jaw. He dropped by the water's edge and lay with his cheek in mud.

Gasping, Matt stood looking down at him. Then he heard Sam's voice on the bank above, almost prayerful with delight.

"I heard him run this way an' followed him," Sam said. "His men scattered out and didn't wait to get corralled. I guess this settles everything, don't it, Matt?"

"Everything," Matt mumbled through swollen lips.

But he was not quite right. Three weeks later, as Sam and the first rafting crew floated through the open boom toward the Mississippi current, Matt shouted from the bank: "Tell Judge Vickers I'll be downriver to call on him!"

"At the bank?" Sam called back.

Matt looked at the crowd of raftsmen gathered on the river's edge, listening. He took a breath and got it across to Sam, out there on the vast and slowly moving raft.

"At his house!" Matt shouted. "Tell him to leave word at his house that I'm coming. You'll be understood."

Fourteen Votes Brand a Maverick

T. T. Flynn did not title this story when he finished it in early September. It was one of several short novels that his agent had pre-sold in advance to Street & Smith's *Western Story Magazine*. His agent sent it in at once and it was accepted on September 20, 1939. The author was paid $400. It was titled "14 Votes Brand a Maverick" when it appeared in the issue dated April 13, 1940.

I

Bob Brule had won the Red Rock election by fourteen votes when the last returns came over the mountain from Esmeralda late in the evening.

He was the new sheriff by the skin of his teeth—and fourteen votes, but there were still plenty of people in the Red Rock border country who would have bet bright yellow gold that no young upstart of twenty-three would ever fill the boots of old Dakota Canfield.

Five minutes after the Esmeralda riders smoked in with their returns and whooped for whiskey, Harmony Redfield hammered on the bar of his Buckjack Saloon with a six-gun and shouted for quiet. The noisy crowd hushed expectantly.

Harmony smoothed the bristling gray hair around his pinkish bald spot, pushed his ample stomach against the bar, and lifted the gun by the barrel, like a hammer.

"Fourteen votes!" he yelled. "An' they was as good as a million! The house sets 'em up, you right-votin' sons-of-guns! Crowd in an' grab your drinks!"

Harmony slammed the bar with his gun and shrill yells turned the celebration loose in front of the long bar.

Bob Brule, wearing his best black suit, stood before the bar shaking hands and feeling a little foolish at being the center of all this attention. And feeling proud and good about it, too.

This welcome, this celebration were better than the hot

bite of whiskey. They took hold of you deep down inside. The hands thumping your back, pumping your arm, the friends, neighbors, and strangers who wished you luck brought a lump into the throat. They liked you, they wished you well, they were behind you.

Bob had promised them a good sheriff, good law if elected. He had promised them the best law the Red Rock country had known for years. Now, as he shook the eager welcoming hands, he again promised man after man that, day and night, Bob Brule would be backing up the sheriff's badge that they had voted him.

Nobody mentioned old Dakota Canfield who had lost the election. But each time that Bob thought of Dakota—and he thought of him often—the broad smile and flush of pleasure left his face.

Bob Brule had not been born when Dakota Canfield was first elected the Red Rock sheriff. Twenty-eight long years ago that had been. Old Dakota had been young Dakota Canfield then. And probably men had crowded around him that first election night as they were crowding around young Bob Brule tonight. They had probably made as much noise and wished Dakota as well.

Back in those days Dakota had deserved it all. Only in these last years, after his wife and son had been killed by an avalanche of spring snow, had Dakota Canfield turned bitter and started to drink heavily. Folks had been sorry for Dakota, had thought he'd get over it. It seemed as if Dakota had always been the Red Rock sheriff, and always would be. Most of the younger men couldn't remember when Dakota Canfield hadn't been one of the best lawmen in the border country.

But Dakota had just grown more bitter, drunk more heavily, until much of the time he wasn't much good for a sheriff. Friends had tried to reason with him. Dakota had shrugged them aside, grown worse, if anything.

Twice the old-timers had voted Dakota in as usual. And now, tonight, was the end of Dakota Canfield—by fourteen votes. And here at Harmony Redfield's bar, with the victory celebration roaring out through the swinging doors, Bob Brule wasn't happy when he thought of old Dakota. Dragging down a boyhood hero didn't make a man feel better.

Harmony Redfield chortled across the bar: "Sheriff, how does it feel?" Then, abruptly, Harmony's face lost its broad grin. Sharply under his breath he warned: "Watch yourself, Bob!"

The celebration was quieting like fire doused by water. Men fell silent, shuffled uneasily, and, as Bob followed their glances, he heard a man say: "Hello, Dakota."

There he came through the swinging doors, Dakota Canfield himself, staggering slightly. He pushed his way to the bar without answering the speaker.

Tall, gaunt, and stooped, white-whiskered stubble rough on his face, the old lawman looked harsh, bitter. His suit was wrinkled, his shirt soiled and rumpled. But the two old wood-handled guns bulked under his coat as usual. The shining sheriff's badge gleamed, brave and bright, on Dakota's vest, as it had ever since Bob could remember. The slight glassiness in his eyes, the slight lurch were the only signs that Dakota Canfield wasn't himself.

Drunk, Bob thought pityingly. *Drunk an' looking for trouble.*

A long step from him Dakota stopped. Men nearest them shuffled quietly back, made uncomfortable by the bitter glower on Dakota's face.

Bob, waiting silently, suddenly had the feeling that all

111

the back slapping, the handshaking hadn't meant so much, after all. Those who had crowded so jubilantly around him were edging away. Their faces were like strangers' faces, blank and watchful as they waited to see what he would do. Trouble was in the air. None of them wanted any of it. They'd voted all trouble to the newly elected sheriff, to Bob Brule.

With a strange, almost lonely feeling, Bob sensed that it would always be that way for a man behind the sheriff's badge. When trouble threatened, the men with the votes, the hearty handshakes would stand critically back to see what would happen.

Dakota spat scornfully. His voice was thick. "Sheriff, huh? Sheriff by fourteen votes! How many votes did you buy an' steal an' have counted twice, you slick-tongued young maverick?"

Bob reddened, forced himself to speak without anger. "I don't want any trouble tonight, Dakota. Look me up to-morrow if you still feel the same way."

"Tomorrow, hell!" Dakota said violently. "Gimme an answer now!"

"I ain't answerin' such talk tonight."

"I'm callin' you a liar! I'm callin' you a thief!" Dakota yelled furiously. "Is that enough to get anything out o' you?"

"Not enough to make an argument with you," Bob said coolly.

"Figger yourself man enough to wear this badge, huh?" Dakota said loudly. He jerked the bright star off his vest, hurled it to the floor between them. "Are you man enough to fight for it? Go fer your gun, damn you! Show these friends of your'n what kind of a man they voted for!"

"I was elected," Bob said shortly. "No need of gun work

112

to make it official. If you pull one of them old snap busters, Dakota, I'll be standin' right here with my hands out empty. I ain't got any quarrel with you. I ain't been sworn into office an' I'm not packin' a gun. Pin the badge back. You're still the sheriff."

Dakota flipped out one of his guns. His voice was harsh, grating. "I knowed gun work'd show you up! You can buy votes, you young pup! But you can't buy the kind of stuff it takes to hold down my job. Here's a gun! Here's a chance to show how gutsy you are!"

Bob stood still, hands at his sides. The crowd watched silently.

Bob had the feeling that he'd suddenly been thrown on trial here. On trial before the whole Red Rock country. These men who had helped elect him were now judging him. Before morning their judgment would be out over the range. Slowly he put his elbows back on the bar, shook his head.

"I won't have any trouble with you, Dakota. Put up that gun."

The old lawman was glaring furiously. Every man in the saloon, others crowding outside the swinging doors, had heard Dakota Canfield trying to goad Bob Brule into a fight. But none of them could see now the baffled, defeated look that crept into old Dakota's bloodshot eyes. All they could see was Bob Brule, standing there with his face set, expressionless. Dakota wheeled around to the tense watchers.

"Twenty-nine years I been sheriff!" he said bitterly. "Now I ain't good enough fer a heap of you! You sided with a crooked election an' got yourselves *this!*" Dakota spat again, jerked a contemptuous thumb back at Bob. "Well, you got him . . . by fourteen dirty, crooked votes! An' if you had any sense, you'd know where the crooked votes come from! There he is, still wet behind the ears! Half a man when a real man calls him! A hell of a sheriff! An' a hell of a time you'll have out of it, those of you who ain't lookin' fer a new bunch to be runnin' these parts! An' now to hell with all of you! There's your sheriff! There's my badge! I'm quittin' now!"

II

Dakota staggered again as he headed for the swinging doors. But only once. His stooped shoulders were stiff, straight as he strode out.

For a moment Bob had the feeling that the years had been wiped away and once more Dakota Canfield was the tall, formidable lawman he had been long ago. Then the swinging doors closed behind the old man, and Bob remembered the baffled, defeated look that had come like a tide of despair on the seamed, stubble-covered face. Soberly Bob picked up the badge.

A man near him laughed. Other laughs followed, and derisive comments as men got over their feeling of uneasiness.

"Dakota sure had a snootful."

"You'd think he was married to the job."

"Brule, I thought you was gonna take his gun an' call him!"

"You handled him just right, Bob," Harmony Redfield said from across the bar. "He'll get over it."

Bob rubbed the badge clean against his shirt, looked at it a moment, and laid it on the bar. "Give this to Dakota when he's sober. Guess I'll move along, Harmony. It's been a hard day."

"But we ain't started yet," Harmony protested. "Folks want to see you tonight. You ain't gonna back out on the celebratin', Bob?"

"They'll celebrate as high an' handsome without me . . . after a few more drinks," Bob said with a new twist of cynical insight.

Harmony leaned across the bar and spoke guardedly. "Some of them might not understand it, Bob. They might think Dakota worried you up a little."

"They elected me," Bob said with a shrug. "I haven't changed. Set up the drinks."

Harmony shrugged, too, and hammered again on the bar with the gun. "Side up, men! Bob Brule's buying! What'll it be?"

Under cover of the noisy scramble to the bar, Bob walked into the back room—and kept going. Outside in the clear, bright night he paused, thinking. The wind cooled his flushed face, the night peace relaxed his tensed muscles. But there was nothing to bring order to his feverish thoughts.

You could bet some of them would be wondering if Dakota Canfield hadn't backed down the new young sheriff. They'd talk, speculate; the story would twist and grow until all the Red Rock country would be wondering. Chances were that sooner or later some outlaw, some gunman would decide that old Dakota had been right and would make a test.

A man had come quietly out of the back of the saloon. He joined Bob and spoke guardedly.

"I saw you ease out this way, Brule. You aren't letting that old whiskey soak get under your hide, are you?"

Bob recognized the precise set of the gray hat, the smooth, confident rasp of the voice. This was Arch Hayes, the lawyer, who handled the law as cynically and successfully as he played poker. Once Bob had heard Hayes say that the law was better than poker because you could break the rules easier.

"I'll handle Dakota," Bob said shortly.

"Sure, you will. You're smart," Arch Hayes agreed easily. "Have a cigar?"

"Nope."

"I forgot, this is your day to be passing out cigars instead of taking them." Hayes chuckled. He lighted the cigar he had taken from his coat pocket. The match flare showed his eyes narrowed above smiling lips. He fell into step when Bob moved away through the darkness.

"Canfield will stir up talk," Hayes remarked in a confidential voice. "But just remember you're the sheriff. Nobody can do anything about it."

"That," said Bob slowly, "sounds like advice bought an' paid for across your desk."

Arch Hayes chuckled again. "The bill won't come to you."

"Will there be a bill?"

"I never worry too much about what'll come up tomorrow," Hayes said easily.

"You don't seem to mind advising about what might happen tomorrow," Bob commented. "You make me wonder who might want to do anything about my being sheriff."

"Dakota Canfield still has friends," Hayes reminded.

"That's right. I'd like to be one of them."

"You have friends," the lawyer said coolly. "We elected you. We'll be backing you all the way."

116

"Now that's nice."

"It might be nice to know."

"Just who will be backing me up?" Bob asked innocently.

Hayes hesitated. "La Plata Cattle Company for one."

They had been walking down the alley, were almost at the cross street when Hayes said that. Bob stopped and peered at the lawyer.

"So it's the Plata bunch? I couldn't figure who'd have a bill for all this. Maybe you'd better get me straight, Hayes. You'll hear it later, anyway. Gurnee Silver's La Plata Cattle Company don't an' won't mean any more to me than anyone else. Gurnee Silver will do well to stay around his Mex *haciendas* over the border if he wants special treatment. I hear that Silver's at the Circle Dollar now. You might take word out to him quick so he won't have any doubt."

"I might . . . but I won't, Brule. It'll do you no good to let Silver know you're thinking like this."

"I'll tell him myself then," Bob declared.

"Better not," Hayes advised coolly. "Silver might change his mind. Who do you think put you in office anyway?"

"I figured my friends did."

The night hid Arch Hayes's face, but his voice was amused. "Your friends helped some, Brule, but you're a long way from having as many friends as Dakota Canfield. He's had almost thirty years in office to tally friends. You're just getting started. Things like that count in elections. You skinned by with fourteen votes. If it hadn't been for Gurnee Silver, you wouldn't have had a chance."

Bob swore softly. "So Dakota was right? There *was* dirty work." He caught the lawyer's coat lapel and jerked him close. "*You* did Silver's dirty work behind my back. *You* made a crook an' a thief out o' me just like Dakota said."

117

Arch Hayes did not make the mistake of struggling. He stood with the cigar glowing between his fingers and his coat all bunched up in front. His voice was cynical: "Don't be a fool. Nobody can prove anything against you. If you hadn't looked like a good man, someone else would have been put in to run against Canfield. And that man would have won. Gurnee Silver wants a good man as sheriff. He figured you were the best bet. You're young. You're set for life if you make the right kind of a sheriff. Isn't that what you want?"

"What kind of a sheriff?" Bob asked in a strangled voice. "I'll tell you, damn you. *Your* kind of a sheriff . . . with Gurnee Silver's blindfold over my eyes an' your hobbles on my feet. Damn you both. A loaded six-gun couldn't settle what you two have done to me today."

His right fist smashed into Hayes's mouth. The blow made a squashed soggy sound and the jolt of it went clear back to Bob's shoulder as the lawyer sprawled on the ground.

Hayes rolled over, came up to a knee. His voice, low and strangled, shook with rage and sounded thick, as if his lips were mashed and numb. "I've got a Derringer here! Put a hand toward me again, Brule, and I'll kill you!" He staggered to his feet, backed off a step. A shrill note of wild fury blazed in his voice. "You damned young fool! I ought to kill you, anyway! Maybe it'll have to be done! But I'll give you a chance to think it over. And listen to me, Brule. If you've got a fool idea of making a move about this tonight, remember there's no proof to back you up. I'll deny all knowledge of it and there'll be enough men to swear that *you* paid them for their votes. *You,* damn you!" Hayes choked, sounded as if he were spitting blood from his mouth. The same shrill note of fury gave a raw edge to his

118

voice. "You'll take the blame for any talk you start. If you get some sense, I'll still show you how you're lucky to be sheriff. Now stand there while I leave."

He backed toward the street. There wasn't any doubt that he'd shoot at the slightest excuse. But he needn't have worried. Bob Brule stood there, feeling sick and helpless. Hayes was right! They'd set a crafty trap and sprung it cleverly. Who would believe now that Bob Brule hadn't known all about the crooked work that had won him the election? Who'd believe he had taken that tongue lashing from old Dakota when it wasn't true?

Hayes was gone now. The clear night seemed darker, abruptly lonely. Bob had been lonely before this, lonely many times since the days when he was only a button out on Dee Kline's Running M outfit. But there had always been friends. Now how many friends would there be when word spread that Bob Brule had crooked old Dakota Canfield out of the election?

III

The Gunsight Hotel bar was crowded, too. The noisy clamor was spilling out open windows. Some of the bunch in there would be celebrating Bob Brule's victory. Some would not. Bob didn't want to see any of them. He entered the hotel from the rear and walked up the back stairs to his room.

A look in the mirror as he pulled off his black coat showed his face set and pale. The smear of crimson on his knuckles would be from Arch Hayes's smashed mouth.

Bob dipped water into the tin washbasin, washed the

hand, shucked out of the suit into Levi's, leather vest, and old coat. From a drawer he took a scuffed gun belt and an old wooden-handled six-gun.

Dee Kline had given him the gun on his fourteenth birthday.

"Your old man was handy with this 'un," Dee had said. "But the last time he drawed, he was a mite too slow. You better learn all about it early, bud. A fast gun hand never hurt ary peaceable man . . . but it's shore helped many a one."

Some of the cartridge loops were empty. From a box of cartridges in the same drawer, Bob filled the empty loops, dropped the rest into his pocket. Then he left the black suit hanging in the room, left the hotel by the back way again, and cut over to Tom Shade's stable, where his rifle, saddle, and horse were.

Tom Shade wasn't around. The hostler was a shifty-eyed Mexican called Pacho. Talk said Pacho was a heavy gambler among the local Mexicans, winner most of the time, and a bad man with a knife. Bob had never liked him.

Now Pacho lounged under a smoky lantern in the stable doorway and grinned. "How eet feel to be the new shereef, *Señor* Brule?"

"I ain't sheriff yet," Bob said briefly. "But after I am, *hombre*, don't drag your knife in a fight. It'll be the *carcel* for you fast."

Pacho showed white teeth in a wider grin. "Oh, *sí*. I am leetle white woolly lamb now. *¿Verdad?*"

"I ain't sure just what you are," Bob told him curtly. "Bleatin' about it tonight won't make up my mind. Saddle my horse."

Pacho lingered with a thin smile. "I vote for you, *señor*. *Mis compañeros* vote, too. We all don' forget that, no?"

An hour back Bob might have grinned, thanked Pacho. Mexicans born north of the border voted as well as any man. Now Bob's eyes narrowed. Arch Hayes had put the meaning of Pacho's sly look into words. The anger on Bob's face sent the hostler back an uneasy step.

"Saddle the horse," Bob said thickly.

"¡Sí, sí!" Pacho snatched down the lantern and hurried back into the cavernous barn.

Slowly Bob opened his fists. Arch Hayes had done this to him! Backed by La Plata outfit, Arch Hayes had fixed it so that a shifty Mexican could grin knowingly at Bob Brule. Whipping the Mex wouldn't help. Make it worse, if anything. Bob made his decision standing there, and turned on his heel. He walked with long, angry strides to the corner and turned toward the Gunsight Hotel.

A joyous waddy yelled loudly, crashed gunshots toward the stars from the middle of the street. Watchers smiled or ignored the shooting. Red Rock was celebrating.

Bob wondered how many in town knew what Arch Hayes knew? How many suspected and would never say? He couldn't be sure who was his friend now, and who was just stringing along with the new sheriff.

The wild drum of hoofs entering Red Rock from the north, wilder yells, blasting crescendo of handguns swung Bob around to watch. He had an idea who was coming. He was right.

They came out of the night with a rush, yelling, emptying their guns. Eight or nine riders, closely bunched, range-blackened by sun and wind, hard, fit, sure of themselves. No ranch in all the Red Rock country could send a better bunch of men to town. Top hands all, forking fine horses, fine saddles, dressed colorfully.

They were La Plata Company men, Gurnee Silver's

men, brought north from his ranches in old Mexico. Scratch any one of them and you'd find a top rider and gunman. You'd find a man who knew he was good and was ready to prove it at the drop of a hat. They were like Gurnee Silver himself, bold and sure of themselves. Men who rode for Gurnee Silver had to have some of that hard-bitten, two-fisted drive that had sent Silver himself as a young man over the border with his guns and horse to marry the daughter of a small Spanish *haciendado,* and had carried Silver on to wealth and property such as few Yankee cowpunchers had ever collected.

Only Gurnee Silver could tell how he'd gotten the ranches, the cattle, the mines, and other properties he now owned. The great, laughing, domineering hulk of him had found Mexico to his liking. He had gotten what he wanted and held it with hard-fisted, fighting ownership. His son, Tony Silver, was a copy of what the old man must have been in his younger days.

Two years back Gurnee Silver had looked at the changing times and decided he needed grass north of the border. His La Plata Company had bought Red Rock land and started to expand. No man had sold his property to La Plata Company for less than it was worth. There was agreement about that. But when a man refused to sell, he found himself in trouble. Fences down, haystacks burned, border jumpers running off his stock. No one could prove that Gurnee Silver's hand touched any of the trouble. Silver himself spent most of his time south of the border. Those ranchers who came to the point of selling got dollar for dollar for all they'd owned before trouble hit them. They got their money from Arch Hayes, the Red Rock lawyer, or a laughing, booming, self-confident Tony Silver, who had been put in charge of new La Plata holdings.

This year a great ranch house had been started out on La Plata land here. There were rumors that Gurnee Silver had gotten in bad with the Mexican *politicos* and was getting out while he could. All kinds of talk. Meanwhile, La Plata holdings were growing fast, the big ranch house was almost done. Gurnee Silver, his wife, and daughter had come north with a wagon train of household furnishings and personal effects to install in the big house.

Tonight Tony Silver led La Plata riders in their wild ride to the Gunsight rack. His booming laugh lifted above their loud talk as they hitched in the dust of their coming and swaggered inside. Few greetings were given them by the Red Rock men standing about. Bob noted more than one scowl after La Plata men had disappeared inside. A man sighted Bob, whooped and grabbed for his hand.

"Howdy, Sheriff! We been lookin' for you! It's your night to get ory-eyed!"

Bide Miller was the speaker, a bluff, good-natured young fellow who ranched the Bar W to the south along the Big Chipaya Draw. Others were feeling the same way Bide did, reaching for Bob's hand, slapping his back.

"I'm too busy right now, boys," Bob told them. "Anybody seen Dakota Canfield?"

Bide Miller threw him a quick, inquiring look. "Canfield?"

"That's right."

They'd all heard about his brush with Dakota. You could see them wondering if there were going to be trouble, after all. Bide shrugged.

"Dakota was down the street a couple of hours ago," he said. "It'd be a guess where he is now. Might be inside. Have a look an' a drink with the boys, Bob. It ain't every night we're drinkin' to luck like this."

Andy Anderson, the fat, mournful little bookkeeper in the bank, and owner of shares in several small bunches of cattle, said: "Luck ain't a name for it, Bob. We're lookin' for you to hang a spade bit on some of these border dodgers that have been raising hell around these parts lately."

Bob nodded gravely. "I said I would, Andy . . . if I put on the sheriff's badge. I'll look in here for Dakota and have that snifter. Maybe it'll wash some of the dust out of my eyes."

"Dust in your eyes?" Andy joked.

"That's right," Bob said with a touch of the new grimness that he'd been trying to keep from them. "I'll buy the drinks, men."

That was enough to bring them trouping noisily inside. The barroom was crowded. The bar lined with men. Bob looked around while drinks were being ordered. Dakota was not in sight.

"Seen Canfield lately?" Bob called to the barkeep who was setting out bottles and glasses.

"Not short of an hour." The man shrugged. "Oughta see him in here most any time now. He's makin' the rounds tonight."

Tony Silver and his Plata men were bunched near the center of the bar. And it was Tony Silver who turned, laughing, with a whiskey glass in his hand.

"Forget Canfield, Brule. He's done. You're the *hombre* who counts now. Side us in a drink. We're for you."

He had the blue eyes and laughing bulk of the graying giant who was his father. And he had black hair and a fine-drawn litheness that must have come from his Spanish mother.

The Spanish in this Tony Silver might account for the dusty white sombrero, the gaudy embroidery on his leather vest, the big-roweled Mexican spurs of hand-beaten white silver. His manner seemed to take it for granted that the new sheriff would be glad of approval, glad to drink.

"Drink with *you?*" Bob said with a rush of tight-lipped bitterness. "Hell, no. I ain't got that low yet."

IV

It took a second for men around them to realize what had been said. Tony Silver himself kept smiling for an instant. Then explosive tension struck every man within hearing. Those nearest Bob began to edge away. La Plata riders around Tony Silver moved out in hard-eyed watchfulness.

La Plata men weren't looking for trouble from Bob Brule. They were leaving him to Tony Silver and were watching the other men in the barroom. Like a wolf pack facing all who did not run with them, Bob thought.

The quick silence spread to the far corners of the room. Nervous movements of the crowd were not loud enough to cover the sound of Tony Silver's drink pouring on the floor. Then the glass made a sharp little impact on the wood and rolled away. Silver's smile was suddenly an angry scowl.

"You're a damn talky *pelado*, Brule," he said roughly. "Shuck off that gun. Let's see what's back of your talk."

His hand started to his gun belt. Bob's hand was on his gun before he saw that Silver wasn't drawing. A sneer spread on the young man's dark, handsome face as he unbuckled the belt and handed it to the Plata man on his right.

"Don't be so jumpy, Brule. I'm only going to whip some manners into you."

That was the hot rough blood of Gurnee Silver that took what was wanted because its owner wanted it.

Bide Miller muttered a warning just back of Bob's shoulder.

"I've heard he's hell in a fight, Bob. Don't let him egg you into it."

Bob thrust his belt and gun back to Bide without answering. No one paid any attention to the bartender's protests. Tony Silver swept his white sombrero behind him and leaped, striking hard.

He was half an inch taller, pounds heavier, faster than the bulk of him looked. He missed the first blow, plunged into Bob, slammed the other fist against Bob's cheek as they stumbled across the room.

"Anyone who butts in gets hurt!" That shout came from La Plata's *segundo*, Hooker McReady, who had come north with the first Plata men. The warning was not needed. Nobody was interfering. Men backed against the walls and bar to watch the fight raging across the room.

Bob took a blow on the chest that stopped his breath. He smashed a fist to Silver's mouth. They circled and jumped at each other again. Silver's mouth was bleeding. Wild anger flared on his face as Bob hit him twice more and jumped back.

"Show him, Bob!" Bide Miller yelled.

Bide's yell was still in the air when Silver closed with a rush of fury that beat Bob's guard down, carried him, stumbling, back against chairs and a table. The chairs went over, the table reeled back. A smash knocked Bob to the floor.

Tony Silver bellowed, jumped to stamp him. Bob rolled desperately. The Silver temper was raging, and it was doubtful whether Tony Silver now knew or cared what he was doing.

A boot just missed Bob's head. Sharp spur rowels slashed his cheek. Then as he rolled, his hand caught a table leg, slung the table against Tony Silver's hip. That gave him a moment to scramble up, to back off with the bite of pain in his slashed cheek clearing his head.

Bellowing again, Tony Silver dashed the table aside and plunged after him. The man was muscular, fast, more dangerous even than he had seemed. Bob dodged—and then came back as Tony Silver whirled after him.

A hard right knocked Tony Silver back on his heels. Bob followed it up with a left and another right, grunting with the desperate effort of the blows. He knew he was done if Tony Silver got him down again, through as sheriff anyway, branded crooked in all the years to come by the Silvers and Arch Hayes.

The bitter fire of it drove him after Tony Silver now, sledging blow after blow that kept Silver off balance, carried him back and back the length of the long barroom. Tony Silver had stopped bellowing. They were both silent, save for gasping breaths and grunts as they hit and were hit back. The crowd was silent, too, as all eyes riveted on the fight raging down the room.

Some of the men might have sensed that this was more than a barroom fight. This was the first time the Silvers had been challenged openly in the Red Rock country. This was as good as old Gurnee Silver himself being battered before their eyes.

Tony Silver was too ragingly stubborn to dodge, too groggy to catch balance and make a stand. Step by step, he went back before the smashing, slashing blows that had no end.

Both men were tiring fast. It couldn't keep up. Tony Silver's face was battered, bloody. Bob was bloody, too. His arms felt numb, strength was leaving his body.

Hooker McReady's harsh voice sounded far off. "There's been enough of it! Stop 'em both!"

"You wanted it this way!" Bide Miller charged angrily. "I'll pull a gun on the man who butts in!"

The angry cries of assent meant little to Bob. The ranks of men crowded back against the walls; the barroom itself had vanished from his vision. Only Tony Silver's cut, bleeding face before him mattered, that face at which he was throwing fists as fast as weary arms would move. He was hit back, but he was past feeling the blows.

Men standing before the swinging doors got out of their way. Tony Silver staggered back through the doors into the hotel lobby where others had gathered, and still more were coming in from outside as news of the fight spread.

Tony Silver rocked on weaving legs and swung wildly. He missed. Bob hit him again with all his strength. The sodden shock of the impact went through his body. Tony Silver reeled around and fell hard.

Sobbing for breath, he tried to crawl to hands and knees.

"Stomp him, Brule, like he tried to stomp you!" someone yelled.

A swirl of skirts darted in front of Tony Silver's blood-smeared face. Bob looked up dizzily into the delicate oval of a girl's face that was flushed with anger and scorn as she cried at him. "Don't dare try it! He's helpless! Can't you see he's helpless?"

The big man who swung her away from the spot by an arm addressed her in a cold, angry voice. "Keep out of this, Judith. Your brother don't need to hide behind a woman's skirts."

He must have been watching, Gurnee Silver himself. Gray was in his mustache and hair. He wore fine riding boots and an expensive broadcloth suit. The gun that talk said never left him showed an ivory handle inside the open coat. Blue eyes in a dark-tanned face were coldly challenging.

"Finish it!" Gurnee Silver ordered as he stepped back.

Tony Silver was staggering up again, shaking his head dazedly.

"He's had enough," Bob panted.

Gurnee Silver's rage showed itself in a roar. "Who said he's had enough? Tony, are you through?"

Tony Silver replied by staggering forward. And Gurnee Silver stood there like a man of rock while Bob smashed one final blow that reached Silver's chin. This time Tony Silver sprawled limply on the floor.

V

Bob caught Judith Silver's eye. Pale as she was and hurt over the hurt of her brother, she was the most beautiful girl he had ever seen in Red Rock. She had the delicate mark of her Spanish blood, the blue eyes of her father and brother. Her look at Bob had the cut of a riding whip.

"Going to stomp him?" Gurnee Silver demanded harshly.

"No," Bob said thickly.

Gurnee Silver's face was still hard and expressionless as he called to his *segundo:* "McReady, when Tony can walk, start him home. He's had his town fun for tonight."

Bob turned to leave. Silver's voice stopped him. "You're the new sheriff, they tell me."

"Dakota Canfield's the sheriff, damn you," Bob said

129

bleakly. "Does that mean anything to you?"

"No," denied Gurnee Silver. His face remained rock-hard, did not change expression when Bob shouldered past him toward the stairs, ignoring the men who would have spoken to him.

Bide Miller hurried after him.

"Glory be, you shore made a mess of him, Bob. I wasn't lookin' for you to do it."

"He's game, for a low-down skunk," Bob mumbled through split lips as they started up the stairs. "What'd he do to me?"

"You look like a trail herd stampeded over you," Bide admitted after a critical look. "Lemme help you. Guess you're dead on your feet."

"I'll do," Bob said. "Look around town for Dakota Canfield, will you? Soon as I'm washed up, I want to see him."

"More trouble?"

Bob grinned crookedly as they paused at the top of the stairs. "You might say so. It won't be a fight, though."

"None of my business." Bide shrugged. "Where'll I find you?"

"I'll wait in my room."

"Good idea," Bide agreed. "You stamped in a nest of rattlers when you whipped old Silver's son. Ain't you heard talk how Gurnee Silver figures the sun rises an' sets in that wild young bull of his'n?"

"Damn all the Silvers."

Bide shook his bead. "You're sure proddy about 'em. For no reason at all you pick a fight with the whole Plata bunch. An' they stay on the prod, ready for trouble. No telling what would have happened if they all hadn't figured you'd get stomped short and fast." Bide shook his head again. "It ain't the easiest way to start out being sheriff.

There's trouble ahead. Wasn't a month ago that Tully Williams had half his cattle run off, and gave up and sold to Gurnee Silver."

"I know," Bob said. "Williams got all he figured the place was worth, didn't he?"

"Did you talk to Tully about it?" Bide countered.

"No," Bob admitted.

You've got some to learn, even if a lot of us figure you'll make a good sheriff," Bide Miller said with a darkening face. "Bob, Tully Williams came there by Sand Creek thirteen, fourteen years ago. Fenced his water with his own two hands. Built the house himself. His wife helped run their little bunch of cattle the first couple of years. Their kids was born there. They nursed up the beef herd, fenced more land, built more on the house, an' got the place fixed like they wanted it to grow old on. They liked the country and the friends they had. They wasn't interested in gettin' what the place was worth. Tully an' his missus had things there that money wouldn't buy them. An' then they had to sell out, pull up, an' start all over again somewheres else."

"Too bad," Bob said heavily.

"It's worse'n that," Bide Miller growled with sudden passion. "It's got to be stopped. Damn Gurnee Silver an' the money he's willing to pay for a man's home. We've all got a right to ranch and live like we want without being crowded out an' bought out by a half Mex land hog who's took a fancy to our homes."

"That's right," Bob agreed.

"Sure it's right!" Bide said passionately. "That's a how-come you got so many votes. I ain't the only one who's expecting trouble. Tully Williams wasn't the last one that's gonna be forced out. Gurnee Silver ain't got half the land he wants. Arch Hayes has said so. We need a sheriff from now on who'll hit the saddle when trouble shows up and keep going until this country is bad medicine for trouble-makers." He struck a hard fist into a rough palm and went on harshly. "We aim to keep the homes we've got. There'll be enough of us to back you up. If it means a showdown fight with Gurnee Silver an' those hardcases who ride for him, we'll side you on it."

"Your land is next to the ranch that Tully Williams sold," Bob murmured thoughtfully.

"I had my offer before Tully got his," Bide said grimly. "I'm lookin' for trouble any time. And if it happens, and you ain't took over the sheriff's office yet, ride like you are the sheriff. There'll be enough of us to back you on it. We're finished with old Canfield . . . an' he's give public notice he's through with the office. I rode in today to see how you made out an' to have a talk with others about what's to be done."

"I'm not the sheriff," Bob said soberly. "I won't be the sheriff. I'll ride with any of you small ranchers who set out to stop this trouble. But I'm giving the election back to Dakota as soon as I get him sober enough to understand cold talk."

"You got punched crazy in that fight!" Bide said violently.

"I was looking for Dakota before I ran into Silver."

"It don't make sense!"

"Plenty of sense," Bob said bleakly. "To me, anyway."

"By damn," said Bide, staring, "are you gettin' cold feet over Gurnee Silver an' those Plata riders?"

"Call it that if you want to."

"I'm not callin' it that," Bide snapped. "But there's plenty who will. You're double-crossing the men who counted on you. They could have tried to elect someone else. Now there ain't a chance. They'll be worse off than ever if you run out an' give it back to old Canfield."

"It's got to be that way, Bide."

"Then I'll get my say in before anyone else!" Bide exploded. "Either you've been bought by Silver or you've turned yaller! To hell with you, you dirty double-crossin' skunk! And if you want to stay healthy, get out of these parts on the run. Every man you've throwed down will be itchin' to take a sight on you."

"I'll be around," Bob said quietly, but Bide Miller was already going down the steps two at a time, his face black with anger.

Bob swore heavily under his breath. He went to his room, scowled at what he saw in the mirror, poured out water, and did the best he could in the way of repairs.

He still looked bad enough when he left the room and went down through the front of the hotel. The Silvers were gone. A man or two nodded. Several grinned crookedly. Others stared with bleak, hard faces as he walked out. Bide Miller had spread the word fast.

Groups of men stood around out front. Most of them cowmen, many of them men who had promised him their votes. A strained quiet fell over them as Bob appeared, and he knew they had been talking about him.

Bob nodded at them and turned toward the feed barn—and sensed as he did so that he was going to be stopped. Ed Vance, who was partner with Andy Anderson in a small beef herd, was the one who blocked his way. Vance's short dark beard hid the look on his face, but his manner was surly, his voice harsh.

"What's this we hear about you givin' the election to Canfield?"

"You heard it all, I reckon, Vance."

"*You* ain't heard it all, though," the rancher said angrily. "I didn't believe it, but I guess it's so. You've sold us out,

Brule, throwed us over. Why, damn your dirty. . . ."

"Git out of the way, Vance," Bob warned. "I'm in a hurry an' I've had all the fight I want tonight."

But Ed Vance stood there, burly, hard, threatening, and his voice lifted furiously. "He's in a hurry, men! Rushin' around to get shut of everything an' leave us holdin' the bag! Are we gonna lay back an' get laughed at? Gonna let this smart jack deal us from the bottom of the deck an' ease off grinnin' to hisself? He never had no intention from the first of sellin' us anything but a double-cross!"

"His neck oughta be stretched!" called someone back in the shadows.

It was like a spark to powder. Another voice yelled: "Who's got a rope!" Someone else took it up: "Run him out o' town an' call it good riddance!"

Bob wouldn't have believed it possible. Some of these men had shaken his hand, slapped his back, wished him well only an hour ago. Now they were ugly and close to a point where a lynching would seem reasonable.

Bob started forward. Ed Vance pushed him roughly back and drew his gun. He never knew what happened next. Not more than a man or two around the spot saw Bob's gun streaking from the holster, barrel flashing up into Vance's dark beard. The sodden impact of the blow wasn't audible. Vance made no sound as he collapsed.

VI

Bob grabbed the nearest man by the shoulder, buried the gun muzzle in his ribs, and backed against the front of the hotel. "Stand back, you fools!" he shouted at the crowd of men. "Do you want a killing here?"

"What happened to Vance?"

"He kilt Vance!"

"Hell, there wa'n't no shot!"

But men fell back from the threat of Bob's gun, milled uncertainly from the spot where Ed Vance lay crumpled and motionless.

"Stand still!" Bob grated at the man he held for a shield. It was Obie Peters, a cheerful, good-natured waddy who had turned as sullen and threatening as the others. "Vance'll be all right," Bob said harshly. "Git back while I walk Obie down the street. There won't be a hangin' to-night without a shootin' first. It ain't worth it if you got any sense left to think. Git back! I'm walking!"

Someone in the growing crowd cursed him. But the men nearest his iron kept hands away from their guns and held back. They needed a leader and no one was willing to take Ed Vance's place.

A prod with the gun started Obie Peters walking. The men ahead of them fell away and they got clear of the crowd.

"You're done in Red Rock, Brule! Keep goin'!" someone called contemptuously.

But no one followed them. They reached the corner, turned toward the feed barn. Bob took Obie's six-gun.

"I'll leave this at the stable, Obie," he said. "Tell them I don't blame them. I feel worse about this than they do. Maybe Dakota Canfield'll have something to say after I see him."

"T'hell with old Canfield," Obie said violently. "You've said all there is to say, Brule. I wisht they'd stretched your dirty neck. Red Rock country ain't for you after this. Better keep ridin'."

He vanished back around the corner. Bob went on to the livery stable. His horse was tied by the door, gun in the saddle leather. Pacho, the Mexican, stood there with a furtive watchfulness as Bob swung into the saddle.

"You are the shereef now, *señor,* no?" Pacho asked meekly.

"I ain't the sheriff," Bob rasped. "Canfield's the sheriff an' he'll keep on being sheriff. What's on your tricky mind?"

"*Nada, señor,* nothing. But I t'ink if you are shereef like *Señor* Canfield say w'en he ride away leetle while ago, maybe you better know how he swear when I spik your name. Maybe hees not mean so good. . . ."

"Wait a minute!" Bob broke in. "Did Canfield git his horse an' leave?"

"*Sí.* "

"Where'd he go?"

Pacho shrugged, gestured vaguely to the west. "That way, *Señor* Brule. Weeth hees pack horse an' guns." He lifted his hands. "*Caramba,* hees face look black *y malo.* Nevair I see heem look so."

Bob looked down at the dark sly face that was seeking favor with the new sheriff. Old Dakota, he knew, kept a saddle horse, pack horse, and a trail pack here at the feed barn ready for quick riding. In past years he had often used them when riding after law breakers. Now Dakota was gone again. It was a good guess that he'd shaken Red Rock dust from his feet for good. Others might have laughed at the idea, but Bob remembered that baffled look of defeat and despair on Dakota's seamed old face.

"He say when he was coming back?" Bob demanded of the hostler.

"No, *señor.*"

"An' didn't say where he was going?"

"No."

Bob fished $3 from his pocket, flipped them to Pacho for the stable bill. He rode out of the doorway into the west. No telling where Dakota was heading or when he'd stop. And he had to be caught, brought back.

"It'll be a hell of a note," Bob said aloud with wry bitterness, "if Dakota keeps going an' there ain't any sheriff left for Red Rock."

West out of Red Rock the narrow, dusty road struck across the rough open country toward the Horsehide Hills, and on beyond the Horsehides to the Paloma Mountains, where a man could ride through the high timber and brush until descending valleys and cañons took him across the border into old Mexico.

Out this way a score of trails and branching wagon ruts fanned out into the ranch country. Dakota Canfield knew them all. One guess was as good as another as to which way he'd go. There wasn't a moon by which to read sign, nor would it have helped much. Ranch riders passed too often over the road.

Riding at a lope, Bob tried to put himself in the old sheriff's mind. Where would a man head in Dakota's place? Would he want to see anyone he knew or try to keep off by himself? The more you thought about it that way, the less answer you got.

Dismounting, Bob struck some matches, tried to read the road sign. A stiff sound wind blew the matches out, but it looked like the fresh tracks of two horses had come this way. He rode on for another hour and looked again where the road ruts crossed the white dry sands of the Arroyo Seco. And when all but two of his matches were gone, he was certain the fresh tracks had not come this far.

One of the remaining matches lighted a cigarette, and, after smoking a moment, Bob followed his hunch. South another hour's ride was Dee Kline's Running W Ranch. Dee, another old-timer, had been in the Red Rock country almost as long as Dakota. And even if Dee hadn't seen anything of Dakota, he'd have advice for Bob Brule, who'd come to the Running W as a fatherless button and still looked on it as home.

It was after midnight when Bob rode up to the familiar old ranch house and stiffly dismounted. Sam and Samson, the two big dogs, barked furiously until they got his scent and came forward, sniffing and whining.

Windows were lighted in the ranch house, which was unusual for this time of night. Dee Kline stepped out, heard who it was, and chuckled.

"You got out here quick with the good news, Bob. Slim Jim rode in a couple hours ago an' said it was all over but the shoutin'. So you growed up to be a sheriff?"

They were in the big-beamed living room now, and Dee Kline stood there in the lamplight, small and wiry for all of his white hair, with a faint smile on his shrewd, kindly face.

"Your hoss must 'a' throwed you," he commented as he took in Bob's battered face.

"Two-legged horse name of Tony Silver," Bob told him briefly.

Dee whistled soundlessly. "Startin' off with raw meat, ain't you, son?"

Bob rolled another cigarette. He was stiff, sore, tired, and dispirited. It was easy to slip back into the rôle that had existed between that friendless button and old Dee Kline.

"I ain't starting off, Pop," he said heavily. "I've been run out of Red Rock. They were itchin' to get a rope around my neck. I ain't the sheriff an' I never will be now."

Dee stepped to a cupboard set in the thick adobe wall, turned back with a bottle and two glasses. "A little of this'll help, son. Sit down an' git it off your chest."

He listened gravely to Bob's account of what had happened during the evening. "What else could I do?" Bob finished bitterly. "Arch Hayes an' Gurnee Silver made a crook out o' me before I knew what was happening. Wasn't nothing to do but back out an' let Dakota have it."

"You did right." Dee nodded. "But you played the wrong card in not tellin' Bide Miller why you was throwin' up the office. Can't blame Bide an' the men who voted fer you fer thinkin' you gave them a raw deal."

"Gurnee Silver's the only one I'm blaming, Pop. I thought I could find Dakota quick, get him sobered up, an' mebbeso both of us let everyone in Red Rock know what had happened."

Dee leaned forward, cupping his whiskey glass. His eyes were narrowed and shrewd. "You wasn't by any chance hopin' to get Dakota sobered up like his old self so they'd take kindly to him?"

Bob smiled sheepishly. "He's been a better sheriff than ever I'd be, Pop. He could be again for another term."

"Uhn-huh," Dee agreed. "The hard-headed old idjit oughta have it, too. When he quits, he oughta quit proud an' on his own say-so." Dee set his empty glass on the floor and rubbed his gnarled hands together slowly. "You're still young, Bob. It's all ahead of you. Big things . . . if you make them big. An' they won't be big if you don't stay big inside. This trouble'll settle down some way. A young feller's life ain't smashed up by one mistake, especially when he's in the right about it." His chair creaked as he reached for the bottle. "Dakota's lived through the big years, son. Done purty well, too. Had a right to be proud of hisself. Us old-timers watched him keep the law in these parts when it was a man-sized job. Injuns an' cut-throat *pelados* from across the border, renegade whites an' plain cussed outlaws swarmed through this Red Rock country lookin' for easy pickin's. Dakota put the fear of the law in 'em. An' then times changed an' he could take it easy with his family an' look back an' be proud of all he'd been through." Dee sighed and poured another drink. "Losin' his wife an' boy busted Dakota up. Old codgers like us live a heap in the past, son. Dakota got so he just didn't give a damn about today as long as he could stay likkered up, livin' in the past with his wife an' son an' them wild years when he was cleanin' up the Red Rock country. It wasn't right. Dakota knowed it, but he had enough stiff-necked pride in what he'd been to think folks would still want him."

"Enough of them did," Bob said.

"Dakota don't know it," Dee said, smiling faintly. "His eyes got opened with a bang today. He didn't like what he saw, either . . . an' bein' the stiff-necked old mossyback he is, he hated hisself an' everybody who's snatched the last of his pride away. He pulled freight out o' Red Rock lookin' fer trouble an' not carin' where he met it."

Bob looked sharply at the old man. "Seems to me you know aplenty about Dakota for a man who ain't left the ranch today, Pop."

Dee emptied his glass and grinned. "Dakota come by here, son, a-pawin' an' a-snortin' about what a crooked, two-faced young rascal I brang up an' sent to Red Rock to lie an' steal an election. We liked to tangled over it before I got the straight of what happened. An' then, after I cussed Dakota out an' he cussed me 'n' you both out, he rode on fer devil knows where, lookin' for more trouble. What you aim to do now, Bob?"

"Find Dakota," Bob answered. "I ain't wanted around Red Rock now. They ain't got a sheriff. Dakota has got to go back an' take what he won fair an' square." He shrugged. "An' then I'll look around."

"Look around, huh?" Dee repeated. "What might that cover?"

Bob shrugged again.

"Gurnee Silver?" Dee guessed.

"And Arch Hayes," Bob said. He had clenched a fist without noticing it. Dee Kline's shrewd old eyes marked the hard, bitter lines that had come on the younger man's face.

"Gurnee Silver's a mouthful fer any man. Any dozen men," Dee said slowly. "If all the stories that are floatin' around about him are true, he's used to comin' out on top. He's got money to throw away. He can hire men killed an' buy men's souls if he's got use fer that kind of trash. He never got where he is today by bluff an' talk. He's a wise old lobo, bub. He's fergot more'n you ever been able to pick up yet."

"He did it across the border," Bob said hotly.

"An' in Red Rock when he wanted an election," Dee reminded softly.

Bob stood up with a bleak grin. "Wrong, Dee. He paid his money an' got nothing. He didn't get a sheriff he can use. He got Dakota Canfield, an' there ain't enough money could be brought out o' Mexico to buy Dakota. He lost there an' he watched his son get whipped tonight." Bob frowned. "I don't know what to make of that, Pop. Silver never lifted a hand to help his boy. Had his gunmen right there an' didn't make a move. Pulled his daughter away when she wanted to protect her brother. Made her stand back, an' stood back himself, and gave me leave to tromp that Tony Silver like young Silver was going to tromp me."

"Huh?" said Dee, standing up. "You don't say? So the old man done that, did he? Don't sound like him. He's a fighter. Always was, from what I've heerd." He shook his head. "Go slow with him, Bob. He'll surprise you when you ain't lookin' for it. An' as fer catchin' Dakota tonight, you won't have much luck. Get out your bedroll an' bunk here tonight. You can trail him tomorrow an' mebbeso ketch him."

"You been leadin' up to this all along," Bob guessed.

Dee chuckled. "It's the smart thing to do . . . an' I raised you to be smart. Your bunk's waitin', son, an' Wong'll have breakfast as usual. A man can ride an' think an' fight a heap better on a full belly."

VII

Dee was right as usual. Bob Brule was a better man for the night's sleep, the ham and eggs, coffee, fried potatoes, and cold pie. Better for the wrinkled, grinning face of old Wong padding around the table and the joshing of Slim Jim, Rawhide, One-Eye, and Danny Jones who made excuses to linger around the saddle shed while Bob tied a light trail pack on a spare horse.

"Just my luck I hightailed out o' town before the fun started," Slim Jim complained. "Young Silver, huh? I'd 'a' give a month's pay to seen it."

"I'd 'a' give a month's pay not to've been in it, by the looks of that face," Rawhide drawled.

If any of them had heard Dakota and Dee Kline in the night, they gave no hint. Bob left the telling to Dee if he saw fit, and stopped only for a word with Dee back of the house before he rode off.

"The older you git," said Dee, squinting against the slanting blaze of the early sun, "the more you learn that movin' easy gits you there fastest, bub. Talk that's said can't be took back. A young hothead can git hisself in over his ears before he figgers how to wade out. Dakota ain't no man's fool when he's thinkin' straight . . . an' you oughta know about Gurnee Silver by now. Enough, anyways. Wisht I could help you more, but it's your game from now on."

"Thanks, Pop," Bob said. "You've helped. You always did help."

Dee Kline, leathery tough little cowman from white hair to scuffed riding boots, was smiling as he shifted into Spanish. "*Vaya con Dios, hijo* . . . go with God, son," Dee said in the Mexican parting that could mean much. There was brightness in his wise old eyes, pride and concern that he would only hint at in Spanish.

"*Padre, mil gracias,*" Bob said as he rode off, and his eyes were bright, too, and near to dampness as Dee's had been.

They'd been closer in that moment than ever before. Dee was satisfied with the boy he'd raised, and concerned over what lay ahead. And yet it was Bob Brule's trouble, Bob Brule's fight—and Dee would wait to see what happened.

Gurnee Silver had been like that last night, Bob remembered. For the first time he wondered if he didn't understand what had been in Gurnee Silver's mind. A father's mind—with his son bloody and losing—but Tony Silver's trouble, Tony Silver's fight—and the old man standing back no matter what he wanted to do.

Fair an' square as Dee himself, Bob mused. *An' I'll bet he was hurt like Dee would've been. Hell! What kind o' hombre is that . . . square on one side an' crooked on the other?*

143

Dakota had ridden south. The tracks of horse and pack horse were there on the dusty wagon trail that led south and angled west five miles to the Salt Cañon crossing, 200 feet down and 200 up on the other side. And there the tracks left the western-running ranch trail and struck across the open range toward the *malpais* belt of raw-gullied greasewood ridges that broke finally on the high-wooded knobs of the Boracho Hills.

Straight as a homing crow, Dakota had struck across the *malpais* in the blackness of the night, traveling fast. *Knew where he was going an' in a hell of a hurry to get there,* Bob thought as the sun lifted, brassy and hot, in the clear blue sky.

It was past noon by the time Bob crossed the *malpais*. His canteen of water was almost gone. Behind him heat waves shimmered over the raw, gouged ridges that fell away to the lower country. He was at the first brush and stunted trees of the Boracho Hills. Ahead of him were wooded ridges and brushy draws. East, this broken higher country rose to the steep forested slopes of the Oro Mountains. West in the purple distance were the high mesas and higher slopes of the Paloma Mountains, the cañons and valleys that sloped southward down to the border. To the southwest was the great grassy trough of the Big Chipaya Draw. And in the east and northeast and south, from the high grazing of the Oro peaks to the northern grass of the Big Chipaya Draw were the lands that Gurnee Silver had gathered under title of La Plata Land & Cattle Company.

The big ranch house was to the east, where the cold foaming waters of Oro Creek came rushing down out of the mountains and a man could stand and look out over an empire of land that broke only against the purple Palomas bounding the western horizon. South in the misty distance there was no higher land to cut one off from old Mexico, where the roots of Gurnee Silver still struck deeply.

To the west and to the south were those lands of Tully Williams, Bide Miller, Ed Vance, Two-Bit Johnson, and other smaller ranchers that were being rustled and hazed until they gave up and sold out to Gurnee Silver. Twice in those first Boracho Hills, Bob lost the trail, dismounted, and searched it out. Half an hour in from the edge of the *malpais*, in a sheltered draw screened by fragrant pines and cedars, he found old Dakota's brief dry camp. No fire, no scraps of food, only sign where the horses had been staked out, and a step away the pressed grasses where Dakota's body had stretched.

The blaze of the sun, white, bright, and hot in these first hours after midday, struck back like fire fragments from the base of a big boulder on the side of the draw. Dakota had hurled a whiskey bottle at the boulder. The pieces had scattered in the short, curly grass. You could guess Dakota's anger when he hurled the bottle. Drunk again, perhaps, after the bitter election day and long, hard night of riding, of brooding on the past and empty future. From this high country a man could look back almost to Red Rock—back almost across thirty years that had faltered and gone. In the south, if a man kept riding, was the border, strange country, strange people, oblivion for a man riding out of the past into the last gray dull years of his life.

Bob was sober as he rode on faster along that scant, almost invisible trail. It was as if he had dealt old Dakota a mortal blow and the bitter, beaten victim was slipping away from him, vanishing into the purple distance where nothing could be done to mend the wrong.

Once, far to the left, Bob thought he heard a gunshot. But when he reined up and held the pack horse still, only the hot brooding afternoon, the throbbing shrill of locusts were about him. The trail went straight ahead. Minutes later he rode on. He wanted Dakota Canfield, not one of Gurnee Silver's riders on La Plata land.

Two miles beyond, his horse snorted, threw up its head. Bob saw the man almost in the same moment, at the foot of a slope just ahead. He was sitting at the base of a pine, tied there to the tree, wrists tied behind, arms and torso bound securely to the tree, and turns of a rawhide string holding a balled gag inside his mouth. Helpless if a man ever was—and it didn't need the gray hat pulled crookedly on the head to tell Bob this was the dusty, disheveled figure of Arch Hayes, the Red Rock lawyer.

Hayes made choked, furious sounds behind the gag as Bob dismounted.

"Take it easy," Bob recommended. "I'm here and what you're tryin' to say don't make sense past that gag, anyway."

Sign was here for a quick glance to read. The trampled print of horses, the marks of feet that had moved around before Dakota rode away. Bob cut the rawhide strings, fished out the soggy wad of handkerchief that had held Hayes mute.

"You didn't shoot first or he'd have killed you," Bob guessed. "He wasn't hunting you, his trail has come too fast and straight. But you've come a long way since last night in Red Rock, Hayes. A long way to be out here on La Plata range for Dakota to cut your sign. How come?"

The lawyer was choking, gagged with the stiffness in his mouth and throat. At last, thickly, huskily, his fury began to spout.

"Cut me loose! I'll kill him! I'll have him hunted down and dragged like he dragged me! Get me on my feet, Brule!"

146

Hayes's lips were still swollen from the blow that had bruised Bob's fist the night before. Despite the hoarse, wild fury of the man, his eyes were still cold and calculating. His suit was cluttered with dust and dirt, torn across the shoulder, and the side of his face was bruised. His horse was gone, the gun holster under his coat empty.

Bob stood considering as he rolled tobacco in a paper. "Dragged you, did he? You look it. An' that's a funny thing for an old whiskey soak like Canfield to be doing. He lived a long time in Red Rock without draggin' a man." He twisted the cigarette end, lighted it, inhaled. "Last night it was me you was a hairline from killin'," he said thoughtfully. "Now it's Canfield. There ain't a rattler in a week's ride of here that moves as crooked as you do, Hayes. I'd like to drag you at the end of a rope myself. You weren't left here to make Canfield feel happy. You weren't riding out here to take the air. Can you think fast enough, Hayes, to make me want to turn you loose?"

The wild fury was still there, but Hayes had it choked back now. His eyes said one thing—cold murder!—and his bruised stiff mouth said another, irritably. "Don't be a fool, Brule. I was riding out here looking for Tony Silver. I missed him in Red Rock last night and missed him at the ranch house today. There's a matter of business I must see him about. I'm the Silvers' lawyer, you know."

"Last night you made that plain." Bob nodded, watching the restless lift of his horse's ears and listening to the strident song of the locusts.

There was something here in the brooding heat and loneliness that was as slippery and elusive as Arch Hayes himself. Danger. Warning to a man who followed old Dakota's trail.

Arch Hayes could well be telling the truth. He *was* La Plata's lawyer. That gunshot Bob had heard was proof

147

others—one man at least—was in this part of La Plata range. But there was Canfield—old Dakota Canfield—as a boy and man had known him, that fiercely proud old husk of a brave and great sheriff. Dakota had tied Arch Hayes to stay at the foot of the slender pine until freed. Dakota had gagged him so there'd be no calling for help. Hayes or any man could well die like this unless the man who'd tied him came back. Then, again, Dakota had pushed Hayes's hat down firmly to keep off the sun.

"Sometimes you drag a man to make him talk," Bob said thoughtfully. "An' you leave him like this until you get back to take him along. I reckon Dakota aimed to come back this way. What would it be he found out from you that made him ride on alone?"

Arch Hayes sat rigidly on the scuffed and tumbled pine needles. His hat was crushed awkwardly over his forehead; his eyes were dark coals. He might have been arguing his own law case with a black and bitter intensity.

"You're the next sheriff, Brule. Canfield is out of his head. Blamed me on sight for costing him the election. Roped and dragged me to try to force me to admit what he suspected. Drew a gun on me and threatened to kill me. He took my gun, left me like this. To die, I tell you! A bullet wouldn't do!" he cried passionately. "Without water and without food for as long as I could last was what he said as he rode off. No matter what you think, you're the gainer out of all this, Brule. I don't know what brought you here, following Canfield, but get me to Tony Silver and you'll be cashing profit from it for years to come. No matter what happened between you and Silver last night, he's a man who'll meet you more than halfway, if you'll let him."

"Damn the Silvers, young and old," Bob said with the edge of his bitterness. "They're no better than you . . . an'

148

you got a slight idea what I think o' you. Dakota's the sheriff. He put you here. I'll leave you here for him, without the gag."

Bob pinched out the end of his cigarette before dropping it on the pine needles. Abruptly he changed his mind.

"No, by damn, I'll take you along on the pack horse. We'll find Dakota an' have it out. This is better luck than I expected."

He should have been watching his horse. Those ears would have been warning. The strident locusts were drowning minor sounds and the carpet of soft needles under the pines made a quiet footing. Arch Hayes must have known while he was talking, must have seen her coming. She was speaking before Bob knew she was there.

"Don't move!" she said. "I'll shoot!"

VIII

Rifle was in his saddle boot, handgun in his holster. She was at his back. The clear scorn in her order came through the shimmering heat and song of the locusts with the same whip-like cut of last night when she had darted in front of her brother.

Bob moved to turn his head. She sat there on a small slim mare, a horse to draw the eye, cream and white, with a snowy white tail—a horse to draw the eye and a girl to hold the eye. Judith Silver—Spanish and Yankee. Blue eyes challenging and her young face lovely behind its angry purpose. She was guiding the horse by the touch of her small knees. The rifle that covered Bob was steady in expert hands.

"This," Bob said evenly, "isn't business for a woman, either."

"Where's Tony?" Hayes called thickly to her.

"They cut over to the south." The pressure of her knee sent the mare slowly forward, circling out a little. "They're not needed," she said coldly. "I can handle this."

"Cut this rope and get me up from here," Hayes urged her thickly.

"The sheriff tied him there," Bob warned. "The law's holding him, ma'am. Better stay out of this."

"I heard you threatening him," she said coldly. "I heard him tell you why he was left like this. To die, perhaps. Last night I saw how cruel you could be to a helpless man. To my own brother. We're not in Red Rock now. We're on Gurnee Silver's land."

"Silver's land, Silver's law?" Bob said, smiling thinly. "But you're not dealing with Mexican *pelados* now, ma'am."

His words brought an angry flush to her face. "I'd respect a *pelado!*" she said scornfully. "Move away from him! Keep away from your horse!"

"Purty," Bob said, regarding her admiringly. "Stubborn an' reckless. You wouldn't shoot me, ma'am, to get this crooked lawyer away from the law?"

She shot. No warning in the angry flush of her face, a slight drop of the rifle muzzle, the blasting report, dirt and grass erupting around his foot, a hammer blow on his foot that staggered him and left the leg wrenched and tingling.

His anger was a red mist for a moment. She'd shot him! Cold-bloodedly, arrogantly, like a Silver, she'd shot him. Then he found by the ungainly way he stood that she'd only shot the heel off his boot.

"Will you get away from him?" she demanded. Her voice shook slightly. The flush had left her face. She was pale, taut, ready to shoot again.

Bob's voice shook, too, with the anger that had all but

blinded him for a moment. "You little fool. That might have smashed my foot. Might have crippled me for life. You tried to hide your brother behind your skirts an' now you do this because you know you're a woman an' safe. I can't shoot you, can't risk hurting you. Take him. He's as crooked as your men folks."

He turned his back on her, walked away a dozen steps, and looked away while he heard her get down in silence and free Arch Hayes. Her words to the lawyer were flat and without emotion.

"They'll be here if they heard the shot. We'd better wait for them."

Hayes was smoothly triumphant. "Let me have the rifle, Miss Judith. Brule's dangerous and tricky. I'll watch him while you find Tony. You're very brave, but you mustn't take any more risk."

"I'm not afraid of him."

"Keep him covered with that rifle while I get his gun," Arch Hayes said hurriedly.

Bob turned. Hayes was starting toward him. Judith Silver was holding the rifle ready.

"Get back, Hayes," Bob warned. "She can shoot like the devil's sister, but I'll get you first."

Hayes stopped. His cold eyes still held murder, but he took a backward step, shrugging.

"I'll take his horse and look for Tony," he said to the girl. "He won't hurt you."

"Don't take my horse, either," Bob said softly.

"Take my horse and find Tony," Judith Silver told Hayes. "He and father and some of the men are off to the south there somewhere. They can't be far."

He rode hard, away from them. Bob rolled a cigarette and lighted it. The rifle was steady in Judith's hands. She was pale, angry again as Bob smoked and stared at her.

"I wish I *were* a man!" she burst out. "I'd give you your chance!"

"What kind of a chance?" Bob asked her slowly. "The chance Gurnee Silver gave me when he bought votes to have me elected, so I'd wear his bridle and bit as sheriff? Making me crooked without my knowledge? The chance he's giving the small ranchers around his land that he's forcing to sell out to him or go broke from rustling and crooked work?"

"You're lying!"

Bob turned his back on her and walked to his horse.

"Don't get on that horse!" she called.

Bob caught the reins, swung into the saddle, and rode away from her without looking back. For tense seconds he expected her to shoot. When she did not, he put the horse into a gallop on the sign Dakota Canfield had left.

He'd gambled that she wouldn't shoot. All her reckless, angry threat had wavered after that one shot at his foot. Regret, something very close to shame, had come like a shadow in her blue eyes. He wasn't worried about her being stranded. His pack horse was there for her to ride. Hayes would be back with her father and brother. And somewhere ahead in these Boracho Hills old Dakota Canfield was riding on business that touched Arch Hayes and Gurnee Silver. You could be certain Dakota hadn't tied the lawyer to the pine tree because of the election. Canfield hadn't left a man helpless to hunger and thirst because of a personal grudge.

The trail showed fast riding. Dakota's pack horse suddenly came into view, tied some miles from where Arch Hayes had been left. More proof that Dakota meant to head back this way, and wanted to ride fast and unhampered.

The Boracho Hills broke down into the lower country. Southwest was the rim of the Big Chipaya Draw. Miles ahead the badlands jutted in from the north. Through here was the fringe of Gurnee Silver's land. Bob realized suddenly that Tully Williams must have owned this land. Bide Miller's ranch lay ahead and to the south, running far out into the Big Chipaya Draw. Dakota's trail was swinging north toward the badlands. And that could mean anything.

Bob's horse pricked inquiring ears. Warily Bob reined up. The locusts were behind. Only the hard breathing of the horse broke the hot silence.

The ears pricked again. Bob heard it then—gunshots, so far in the southwest that they were mere whispers of sound.

Dakota had not been headed that way, unless he'd turned. But trouble must mean Dakota! The whispering shots had stopped. A man couldn't be sure of the exact direction. But the horse was looking to the southwest. Bob made the best guess he could and rode that way.

He reached Sand Creek, a trickle crawling over the sandy creek bottom, looping, wandering through the low hills, and he followed the creek down. All riders in this part of the range would stop along the creek for water.

Then suddenly a bend in the creek showed a saddled horse ahead. Rifle ready for trouble, Bob looked around for the rider. Head up, the horse stood there, looking at him. Reins hung from the saddle horn, rifle was gone from the saddle scabbard.

The horse moved, limping badly, and Bob rode slowly forward. The horse retreated a few steps and waited. It was a gray horse, and, as he rode close, Bob marked a raw furrow, drying blood high up on the left shoulder.

Speaking soothingly, he caught the reins. The sand held tracks where the horse had come to the water, had wandered back to the first grass. No boot marks were visible. The horse was branded Bar W. Bide Miller's brand.

Bob swore softly. "Shot out o' the saddle!" he said aloud.

A man might quarter these brushy draws and hills for days without finding a body, unless the buzzards gathered. Leading the wounded horse, Bob began to puzzle out the back trail.

The horse couldn't have come far. Those whispering shots hadn't been so long ago. He back-trailed to the point where the horse had headed straight for the water. Beyond that point the tracks wandered, finally started to bear out in a vast circle, where the horse had been running.

Then Bob sighted a stumbling figure that fell a moment later, staggered up, stood staring toward him. It was Bide Miller, hatless, coatless, face drawn with pain, a six-gun in his hand.

IX

Bide was standing like a drunken man when Bob galloped up, swung down, and demanded: "Who did it? What happened?"

Bide's scalp was torn above the hairline. Blood had run down into his eyes, streaked his face. Coat and vest were gone, shirt was bloody beside the heart. Pants were bloody between hip and knee, and the bullet hole there was visible.

Bide looked like a dying man. His voice was a hoarse croak, but there was no mistaking the sneer on his blood-smeared face.

Bob caught him, eased him down to the ground. "Save

your cussin' until later, Bide. Did you see Dakota Canfield?"

Panting, Bide sat there. Lips free from blood indicated that the side wound probably hadn't torn his lungs.

"Ain't seen no one but rustlers takin' my best cows," he mumbled. "Forty Rod an' I rode out along the fences. They jumped us. Killed Forty Rod. I got one before they shot me out o' the saddle. I ain't seen your damned sheriff. He drunk an' lost out here?"

Bob hunkered down and met Bide's tortured scorn bluntly. "I don't know what Dakota's doin' out here. I'm trailing him. He left Red Rock last night before I told him he was elected." Bob jerked a thumb back at the Boracho Hills. "I found Arch Hayes back there, where Dakota had tied him to a pine tree an' gone on. Last night Arch Hayes told me he had used Silver's money to buy me votes. They wanted an easy sheriff to handle. Dakota would have won an honest election. That's why I stepped out, Bide, why I'm lookin' for Dakota."

A spasm of pain crossed Bide's face, and, when the spasm passed, his scorn was gone.

"Gurnee Silver again," Bide gasped thickly. "He's got me. He'll git my land now. Crooked votes or honest votes, you're the man for sheriff, Bob. Canfield didn't help Forty Rod an' me. He's a wore-out whiskey guzzler who don't give a damn what happens on Red Rock range. Damn, if I could ride after them . . . !"

"Could you make it home if I put you in the saddle?"

"Doubt it," Bibe confessed. "Might if I was tied on. My horse'd git me there if he was started right." Bide cursed huskily. "They're runnin' my cows to Horse Thief Pool. I hit my head on a rock an' lay there like I was dead. They thought I was dead an' stood talkin' by me a minute. I just had sense enough to hear 'em."

"Horse Thief Pool," Bob said, glancing toward the north. Bide nodded.

"Lemme see them wounds," Bob said quickly. "How's your lungs?"

"Busted a rib an' chewed up some meat on my side. The leg is the bad one."

"Lie down."

Bide gasped with relief as he obeyed. Under the blood-matted shirt Bob found a little blood still oozing. But the splintered rib was the main damage there. It would be hard for a man to ride with that rib, but it could be done if he was gutsy enough.

The leg was worse, a small hole going in, a much larger one coming out. Bone and arteries seemed to have escaped. The ooze of blood was greater here on the leg. Bob swore under his breath at the lack of cloth for a bandage, solved it by jerking off his coat and shirt and slicing the shirt into strips with his knife.

He put a cloth pad over each wound opening in the leg, bandaged them tightly. He needed more cloth, and got it by cutting up his coat.

"Ain't no use to hang all your clothes on me," mumbled Bide.

"You do the groanin'. I'll do the tying," Bob retorted.

Bide grinned crookedly. "You oughta be a doctor. Maybe I can't make it home. You better side me."

"You've got too damned much argument for a dying man," Bob said. "It ain't gettin' home that's worryin' you. It's what'll happen to me at Horse Thief Pool."

"You ain't the man for it," Bide argued weakly. "Keep you from gettin' killed today an' maybe you'll grow into a half fair sheriff."

Bob tied the last knot and spoke with finality. "Climb up on that horse an' I'll get you out o' my way. Damn glad to get rid of you, too."

"No more than I'll be to see the last of you," Bide groaned as Bob helped him up.

They understood one another now. Talk wouldn't change the grim business that lay ahead. Bide would have to take his chances and shift for himself while Bob Brule rode off into worse trouble.

They were swearing, hoorawing one another as Bob boosted Bide on the lame horse, took the saddle rope, and lashed Bide on.

"If you get sleepy and keel over for a nap, lay forward," Bob advised.

Bide's blood-crusted face creased in a mirthless grin.

"If I hang head down, I have nightmares," he said. "I never did like nightmares. Can't eat breakfast after a bad one. Guess I'll try to stay right side up."

"A glutton like you would see it that way," Bob said rudely. "I guess this is the best I can do. I'll roll you a cigarette before you start."

Bide eyed Bob's belt gun hungrily. "I'd buy your gun, only you'll need it," he said. "Haven't got a Derringer tucked away anywhere, have you? Bad nightmares make me want to start shootin'."

"You ain't gonna hang head down under that horse and blow your brains out with my gun," Bob said gruffly as he handed up a cigarette and match. "Not havin' a gun might make you stay head up and ridin'." He swung into his saddle. "Everything straight?" he asked.

"Plenty straight," Bide replied, and his voice turned extra husky. "Good luck, feller."

"Same to you," Bob said.

They parted like that. Briefly, almost gruffly. Bide might slip down under the horse and be kicked and dragged to death before he reached help. Bob Brule might meet killer guns and be a corpse before sunset.

X

Bob might have recognized Horse Thief Pool without Bide's telling him. In the *malpais* belt, north of the Big Chipaya Draw, Horse Thief Pool was hidden away in a sullen cañon cut by some ancient stream long vanished.

You could pass within a stone's throw of the cañon and never know it was there. You could ride fast through the cañon and miss Horse Thief Pool if rains had washed away sign leading into the side pocket where a shallow pool of water lay under an overhang of black rock cliff. But if you knew the cañon, you could travel west through the badlands without cutting the skyline. You could water stolen horses and cattle at the pool and make a quick drive for the western mountains without showing dust to any inquiring eyes sweeping the horizon.

Bob found the brush-bounded meadow where the gunmen had jumped Bide and Forty Rod. There in the grass Forty Rod lay, arms crossed over his chest as Bide had left him. Bide's coat and vest were nearby. Bob put on the coat and felt better with the covering.

Beyond the meadow the tracks of Bide's cattle angled north. They'd not be traveling too fast. A long night lay ahead. Bob bore farther to the east, swinging wide of the gunmen driving Bide's cattle.

Bob had ridden hard and fast already today and it was

with reluctance that he pushed the horse harder. He rode with rifle out and ready, eyes searching the broken country.

He might have been alone in all this vast stretch of back range. Once a small bunch of cattle broke back into the brush. Bob stopped, made sure he had not run into Bide's stolen cows, and rode on.

His horse was tiring fast when the last brush and grass gave way to lava ridges, rock outcrops, raw areas of gravelly soil that held little but cactus and scanty tufts of grass.

Then without warning the cañon dropped away before him. Two hundred feet deep, 500 wide, rocky sides sheer in spots, steep slopes of broken tumbled rocks in other places. Bob skirted the edge, found a descending path, rode down, turned west.

Once every year or so a cloudburst made the cañon floor a raging torrent, but in this weather the sands were hot and dry. On the steep rocky sides grew crooked cane cactus, long whip-like stalks of Spanish wife beaters, patches of prickly pear, and occasional gnarled and scattered bushes. When the shod hoofs struck rock, the sound rang sharply. Bob looked for fresh trail sign and found none.

Dakota had not come this way nor had cattle passed since the last big rain.

Bob took each turn warily, scrutinized the bottom of each descending trail. Horse Thief Pool was not far ahead now. Frowning, he wondered what had happened to Dakota.

The last quarter of a mile Bob rode with rifle cocked, finger on the trigger, eyes searching the rocks ahead, the cañon walls and rimrock above. Horse Thief Pool lay in a rocky side pocket that had sloping walls of great riven and tumbled rocks down which a goat might come, but no horse or cow. Cattle and horse sign led into the side pocket that held the pool, all of it old. Bob rode into the frowning side pocket, certain that he was the first rider here this day.

The still, green-blue water of the pool lay under a black, overhanging rock wall near the back of the pocket. Bob dismounted and let the horse eagerly plunge his muzzle into the water.

An old tin can rested on a rock beside the pool. Bob was drinking when a cold, clipped order struck him rigid.

"Stand still! What'n hell you doin' here?"

Hands level with his shoulders, Bob turned his head toward the voice.

Back beyond the wall of over-hanging rock was the steep back of the pocket where great rocks were cluttered, piled and poised haphazardly to the rimrock high above. Some thirty feet up there, between two huge rocks, a rifle barrel moved enough to be visible. Bob made out a face peering over the rifle sights, all but hidden in the narrow space between the rocks.

"Canfield!" Bob exclaimed with relief.

Dakota's hard, cold voice came back. "That's right, damn you! Who you aimin' to see here?"

"I've been looking for you. Thought I'd missed you when I didn't see horse tracks out there in the cañon."

"You're a liar," Dakota said grimly. "No one knowed I'd be here. What kind o' crooked play're you tryin', Brule? Where's your shirt? Ain't that blood on the shoulder there?"

Bob put the water can back on the rock.

"Forty Rod's coat, Dakota. I used my shirt and coat to tie Bide's wounds. He an' Forty Rod met rustlers moving their beef. Forty Rod's dead. Bide was shot up an' left for dead. Two rustlers are headin' toward this water with the stock. Traveling to the Palomas tonight, I guess."

"You alone?" Dakota asked sharply.

"Yes."

"Playin' sheriff already, huh?" Dakota said with huge contempt. "Bustin' in here like a damn' fool, leavin' tracks. You ain't got as much sense as I thought you had."

"I swung wide and rode fast to get ahead of Bide's cattle," Bob said. "Pull in your horns, Dakota. I thought I'd find you here."

"Brule," said Dakota grimly, "you're lyin'. I'm itchin' fer an excuse to shoot. Shuck out the truth before I git riled."

"You're a stubborn old coot," Bob said with forced calm. "Last night I followed you out of Red Rock. I cut your trail at Dee Kline's and followed you today until I came on Arch Hayes. I'm bettin' Hayes didn't give me the straight of why you tied him. It doesn't matter. Gurnee Silver's daughter rode up, lined her rifle on me, and let Hayes take her horse to get Silver and his men. I rode away from her and came after you fast. I found Bide Miller on the way. Did Hayes tell you I didn't know the election was crooked until I walked out of Redfield's bar last night and Hayes told me? Did he tell you I had a fist fight in Red Rock last night with Tony Silver? Did he tell you a bunch of the men who voted for me run me out of Red Rock last night and I ain't wanted back there?"

"I ain't surprised," Dakota snapped. "You oughta been run out long ago, you yellow-livered young squirt. You're here now an' playin' sheriff. Stay here and git the man Hayes admitted he was ridin' to meet. Git them rustlers you're prattlin' about. I'm pullin' out now an' leavin' it to you."

Dakota stood up, worn old hat pulled low over his seamed, scowling face. Bob grinned thinly at him.

"When I heard crooked votes had elected me, I quit,"

Bob declared. "That's why I got run out of Red Rock. Men who had an idea they needed a new sheriff to stop Gurnee Silver's hog trough ways of gettin' new land figured I'd double-crossed them. You got the election, Dakota. You're the next sheriff. Killers an' rustlers are headin' this way. Git 'em, you stubborn old mule, or I'll ride back to Red Rock and take your office, crooked or honest."

Dakota stood behind the big rocks for a long moment. Bob thought he saw the old shoulders straightening a little. Dakota spoke, and a new ring was in his voice.

"So you're admittin' the honest votes elected me? You're steppin' out?"

"Dee Kline'll tell you."

"Get the hell out o' here, then," Dakota said. "I'll handle this."

No whiskey about old Dakota Canfield now. He stood taller there among the rocks. A changed man. A different man. Like Bob remembered him—the old fighting sheriff that had cleaned up the Red Rock country long years ago.

"I'll help you," Bob offered.

"I don't need no help to get a coupla dirty rustlin' gunmen," Dakota rasped. "You'll just be in my way."

Relief was in Bob's grin. No need to wonder what kind of a sheriff Dakota Canfield would make now. No need to wonder whether he had done right by Bide Miller and his friends in backing out of the sheriff's office. Dakota was all the sheriff Red Rock would need.

"It'd help if I was made a deputy," he suggested.

"I don't need no deputy on this, Brule. I'll bring 'em in an' then go for Arch Hayes."

"You're the boss," Bob said, and the ghost of a smile was on his face as he picked up the rifle.

Maybe Dakota wouldn't admit it, not even to himself,

162

but with this business of the rustlers he would wipe out the recent years, the bitterness of the election, by returning to Red Rock once more with prisoners caught lone-handed.

"Good luck," Bob said, and meant it.

He looked up to the rimrock as he said that—and saw against the skyline a man sighting a rifle down.

"Look out!" Bob yelled, lunging to the side.

A thin sharp report rapped through his warning. Wasp-like the bullet screamed by him and slapped loudly against the placid pool. Bob whipped back an answering shot.

A second man, a third, and fourth appeared up there on the rimrock.

Dakota's rifle barked.

"Git to cover, Brule!" the old sheriff shouted.

XI

Bob already was diving for the nearest big rock, and the angry staccato roll of sudden gunfire beat down into the rock-walled pocket. Lead shrilled closely, slapped, smacked against water and rock.

Dakota's rifle barked again. "Got one!" he whooped.

Bob risked death to look. It was like some great ungainly bird taking flight from the rimrock across the pocket. The drop was sheer and far to the first tumbled rocks at that point. The man was plainly visible against the skyline as he plunged into space, arms waving, body twisting.

A rifle fell away from him, fell faster, streaking down. The body followed. A wild, horrible cry rang through the pocket.

Bob looked away as the rifle struck, clattering on the

rocks. He heard the soggy impact that followed.

Gunfire had stopped. Then like a vicious retort a snapping shot knocked rock chips into Bob's face, ricocheted away in a screaming buzz.

Other guns opened up. Men had dropped to cover. A second bullet knocked sand against Bob's leg. He was half exposed. Those high gunmen could see most spots where a man might try to hide.

Bob wriggled desperately around the rock, scrambled up the steep slope to a huge boulder that gave better protection.

"Did you say two rustlers?" Dakota's voice coolly questioned. "They's seven at least, countin' the one I pulled down."

"Bide Miller saw only two."

"Did you say Arch Hayes went to find Gurnee Silver?"

"Yes."

Dakota swore in harsh anger. "Then that's Silver's men up there! Maybe Silver hisself helping to pot shoot us! The dirty border thief!"

Bob saw head and shoulders of a man taking aim down at them, whipped a shot at the spot, saw the man draw back. He couldn't tell whether he'd hit him.

Dakota swore again. "Plumb through my hat! Me waitin' like an old fool down here in a trap like this!"

The men on the rimrock were keeping down out of sight. Bob saw a bush sprout magically on the edge. He marked the spot.

Dakota was out of sight higher up among the rocks. His rifle spoke. He was muttering aloud. His voice lifted to Bob. "I oughta brought Arch Hayes along. Had an idea he was lying about meeting one man here. He knowed Silver was around. But he whined an' bellered so when I drug him a leetle to make him talk, I figgered he didn't have guts to lie an' scheme to my face. I thought I'd just climb down here from above an' ketch whoever Hayes was aimin' to meet here at the pool. An' now look at me!"

Bob saw a slight movement at the new bush up there on the rimrock. He lined sights fast and shot. The bush jerked over—but no man appeared. A screaming bullet tore a furrow in Bob's shoulder before he could get behind cover again.

Now and then they could hear voices shouting up there on the rimrock. The men were moving around the pocket for vantage points where they could sight on the men below.

Dakota swore loudly again. "That 'n' took meat out o' my back! Some misguided son is bouncin' lead off the rock behind me! Are you fixed good, Brule?"

"Somebody's shooting mighty close," Bob admitted.

"See them three big rocks under the overhang back of the pool?" Dakota asked. "Try to make it there!"

Bob made a plunging run up the steep slope. Men shouted on the rimrock. Every gun up there opened fire. Screaming lead ricocheted off the rocks all about him.

Dakota was scrambling for the same three rocks. Bob slipped, and, as he came up, there was a cold, slamming jar in the calf of his left leg. Another bullet grazed his side. Rock chips spattered into his face. Gasping, he scrambled behind the three rocks.

Dakota was already crouching there. His face was bleeding, but his hand was steady as he wrapped a bandanna around his left forearm.

"Chunk o' rock gashed my face. Got a hole in my arm," he said coolly. "How you makin' out?"

"One in the leg," Bob replied, looking up at the black

rock cliff that bulged out slightly above their heads. "They can't get over us anyway," he said. "They were working around to try it."

"Got us trapped," Dakota grumbled. "Serves me right for lettin' it happen. But I wasn't figgerin' on Gurnee Silver an' his gunmen."

Bob looked down the slope to the blue-green pool, uneasy now as lead and rock chips struck the water. Between the three big rocks he could see the skyline where guns searched for them. Ignoring the wounded leg, Bob peered intently, and threw a quick shot at a movement up there.

"Made him jump anyway." He grinned, reaching for fresh cartridges. He looked over to find Dakota studying him. The old man grunted, started reloading, too.

"We'll git more of 'em yet," Dakota said, and looked up at the bulging cliff above as lead ricocheted down beside him. He snorted. "Might 'a' knowed some dirty son'd figure out the one way to get at us here. Bouncin' lead off the rock up there is as good as shootin' around a corner at us."

The guns above them went silent again. Dakota looked at Bob as a shout rang out.

"Brule! Canfield! Do you hear me?"

"That," said Bob, scowling, "is Arch Hayes, or I'm a liar."

"You ain't a liar," Dakota grunted. He cupped his hands and replied: "Ain't Gurnee Silver man enough to speak for hisself?"

Arch Hayes was silent for a moment, and then his reply floated down.

"Silver isn't here! Come out with your hands up and we'll take you back to Red Rock to stand trial for tying me up! Or let you ride out of these parts and keep going! You haven't got a chance down there!"

Dakota spat and answered harshly. "You opened fire on the law, Hayes! I'll outlaw you and Gurnee Silver an' every dirty, gun-totin' rascal I git up there!"

The guns opened fire again. The screaming spatter of lead was all about the two men. Dakota hunched his shoulders as lead particles struck his back.

Bob looked down the rocky slope.

"A man might wade through the back of the pool, Dakota, and make a break out into the cañon," he suggested.

"Your hoss lit out," Dakota retorted. "We'd be two rabbits scuttlin' along the cañon while they hunted us from the top. We'll stick it out here to dark. Better tie your leg. Blood's comin' through fast."

Dakota cocked his rifle, peered around one of the big rocks, and scanned the skyline. Bob did the same. They both saw a movement up there. They fired in the same instant. This time there was no doubt about the convulsive leap of a dying man high up on the cliff edge.

Dakota grinned crookedly. "One more. We're gittin' 'em down to our size . . . if they don't bounce enough lead in our necks to stop us before dark." He reached for a plug of tobacco. "Come dark, if they're still up there, we'll make a bust out in the cañon an' git up there at 'em on even ground. There ain't time to git a posse before they scatter."

Bob nodded, and the faint smile passed again over his face. Gone now was that baffled, defeated look that had come like a tide of despair on Dakota's old face back there in Harmony Redfield's saloon. Alive or dead, the setting sun would find Dakota once more the hard-fighting sheriff Bob Brule had hero-worshiped as a boy.

The guns snarled down at them without ceasing. Now and then they shot back. More ricocheting lead wounded them both slightly.

Then for long moments the gunfire on the rimrock seemed to double. A man sprang into view. Dakota knocked him over with a fast shot.

"Tally one more," Dakota said calmly. A few moments later he scowled. "Reckon Hayes has got another tricky scheme up his sleeve?"

A last ragged burst of shots up there had died away. Brooding silence fell over the shadows gathering in the bottom of the pocket, and then above them a mighty bellow rang from rock to rock.

"Brule, are you down there?"

Eyes narrowing, Bob looked at Dakota. "Gurnee Silver."

"Answer the dirty wolf."

"All right, Silver! What do you want?"

"I'm coming to the edge!"

"Figures he's trickier than Hayes," Dakota said savagely. "I'll bring him down shore as hell's full of cinders if he deals a wrong card."

Gurnee Silver appeared on the rimrock. The setting sun struck bright and golden against his huge figure, broad shoulders, wide sombrero. The bellow of his voice rang down to them again.

"All clear up here now! We've got Hayes and the rest of these gunmen! Is Canfield there, too?"

"You're damned right he is!" Dakota yelled back. "An' I got my sights on you, Silver! Your smooth tricks won't work any better'n Hayes's talk!"

Silver's shout held sudden wrath. "Are you trying to say we've been shooting at you?"

"I'll show you when I ketch up with you!" Dakota promised harshly.

"Hold that gun!" Silver roared.

At the point where Silver stood a man might get down with difficulty over and among the steep-piled rocks. And down he came, Gurnee Silver, big, muscular, agile despite his years. Down, down, without a gun in his hand, and not a trace of fear in his advance.

"By hell," said Dakota. "Give him credit for bein' a man anyway."

They were standing now, rifles cocked and ready as they watched Gurnee Silver come to face them. He wore the same fine riding boots and costly suit of black broadcloth Bob Brule had seen him in last night, but they were powdered now with dust. Face hard, mustache close to bristling, Silver dropped lightly behind the big rocks and faced them. His voice was coldly challenging.

"It's me who told you what happened up there. Gurnee Silver told you."

The hard, rough pride of the big man was like a fist in their faces. Bob gave it back with anger.

"Gurnee Silver. That's why we're looking for a trick. Why didn't you bring Arch Hayes to tell it, too?"

Dakota was a grizzled, bloody old man who stood, straight and watchful, and his words had a cold, quiet warning, strangely more dangerous than Gurnee Silver's bellow.

"I'm the Red Rock sheriff, Silver. Your trick of gettin' crooked votes for Brule backfired. Brule quit when he found out. I cleaned up this Red Rock country once an' you dirtied it again. Dirtied it with the money an' the ways you picked up across the border, any trick that'd give you a strangle hold on this range like you got across the border."

"No!" Silver denied violently.

"You've done the dirt. You're wearin' the brand," Dakota said in the same chill tones. "Murder an' rustlin' has been done today. I've cleaned wolves off this range before, Silver. I'll clean you, too. There it is. Fill your hand."

Watching warily, Bob saw the broad deep chest of Gurnee Silver lift with a great breath—and then relax as the fiery temper of the big man drained away. Into Silver's bold blue eyes, as in the eyes of Judith Silver, came an expression close to regret.

"So it's true," he said heavily. "Everything my daughter told me Brule said to her. And the things Tony admitted he suspected were happening." Gurnee Silver looked at them squarely. The hard bleakness was gone from his face. "I turned most La Plata managing over to my son. Matters south of the border were taking all my time. I wanted land on this range, sure. All we could get. Tony hired this lawyer, Hayes, to help. We had the money. Hayes knew the country and the people. I've had to fight to keep on top down there across the border. Mostly I tried to fight fair. My son took all land that Hayes could get, paid fairly, and asked no questions. I'd have stopped it if I'd known how Hayes was getting some of the land. He worked with my name, my money, to get the strangle hold you speak of, Sheriff. A hold I didn't want." Gurnee Silver gestured wearily. Regret had crept heavily into his voice. "We were always strangers down there in Mexico. I decided to come back, Sheriff. To make a home where we belonged. I wanted friends, neighbors like ourselves. Friends and neighbors like my folks had when I was young. All we had down there in Mexico couldn't make up for it . . . or the lack of it in the lives of my son and daughter." Gurnee Silver made another futile gesture. "Hayes didn't ride to find me this afternoon. He came this way fast. When I met my daughter and heard what had happened, and what young Brule here had charged me with, I got at once all the truth my son

knew. Of votes bought and sold he denied knowledge. I believe him. We followed Brule's tracks, found this man
Miller, heard his story, left a man with him, and rode hard
for here. We cleaned out those gunmen up there on the
rimrock and are holding the ones that are alive, including
Hayes. He'd been riding here to talk with them when you
met him, Sheriff. He made a break this way to warn them
when Judith gave him her horse."

Gurnee Silver shrugged his broad shoulders and spoke
almost sadly. "I can't undo everything that's been done in
my name. But I'll right what I can, no matter what it costs.
Prisoners are waiting up there, Sheriff. I'll be glad to have
you stop for the night at our house, if you will." Gurnee
Silver cleared his throat. "My daughter, Brule, will be
wanting to apologize to you for a great mistake she made.
She said so. And that," said Gurnee Silver, with another re-
gretful gesture, "is all I can do, Sheriff. The rest is up to
you."

Dakota leaned his rifle against the rock and looked at
Bob. "What about it, Brule?"

"Better stop tonight at the ranch, hadn't we?" Bob said
quickly.

"Thought so," Dakota said dryly, as if he might have
known Judith Silver himself. But nothing like that showed
in his calm decision to the big man facing them bleakly.
"Bob's got purty good judgment for a young deputy. We'll
stop with you, neighbor, an' be obliged."

Dead Man's Gold

T. T. Flynn completed the short novel he titled "Dead Man's Gold" in October, 1939. It was the very next story he wrote following "14 Votes Brand a Maverick". Street & Smith's *Western Story Magazine* was determined to change the tone and contents of the magazine to appeal more to mature readers as opposed to young adults. One of the ways in which it was doing this was to hire many of the talented writers who had been contributing primarily to Popular Publications' *Dime Western* and *Star Western* and who accounted for a good deal of the continuing success of those magazines on newsstands. The foremost of these writers were T. T. Flynn, Luke Short, and Peter Dawson—Luke Short was the pen name for Fred Glidden as Peter Dawson was for his brother Jon Glidden—and all three had the same agent, Marguerite E. Harper. She is the one who negotiated an agreement with Street & Smith that guaranteed wordage from all three of these authors. With the issue dated June 8, 1940 the name of the magazine was changed to simply *Western Story*. "Dead Man's Gold" was bought on November 2, 1939. The author was paid $300. It appeared in Street & Smith's *Western Story* (8/31/40).

I

San Rico had had its share of roaring saloons during the big mining days. Now there was only one—Mort Hayden's San Rico Bar, where the early sun slanted through dusty windows into the staleness of last night's beer and whiskey, into the reek of stale tobacco smoke, cheap powder and perfume.

The heavy-faced bartender was drying glasses. A couple of feet away a group was talking before the bar in low voices when a door slamming open at the back of the building caused two of the men to reach for their guns. Back there behind the card rooms someone tripped, then stumbled hurriedly along the passage.

At the bar a bearded man who had reached for his gun swore under his breath as he backed off a step, watching the passage door.

"Hayden," he growled, "what the hell's up?"

Mort Hayden was the tallest of the group, clean-shaven, pink-faced, dressed like a dandy, even at this early hour. He frowned and fingered the cigar he had jerked from his mouth.

"You're jumpy, Crock. Can't be much." The passage door flew open. Hayden shrugged disgustedly. "Doc Middleton."

With a scurrying rush, Doc Middleton came out of the passage, nightshirt half out of baggy trousers, and breasted the bar, breathing hard.

"Gimme a drink! Gimme the whole damn bottle, Four Bits! I'm swearing off! I knew the blasted stuff'd get me someday!"

The Arizona Kid, a bony, sun-darkened young man on Mort Hayden's right, grinned sarcastically. "You walked home last night, Doc. Let 'em drag you out as usual, an' you'll sleep it off like a baby."

Doc Middleton's shaking hand slopped whiskey as he gulped the drink. He was a small man, pudgy and unshaven, with long graying hair and tobacco-stained mustache, cheeks sagging from age and dissipation. His voice had a hard drinker's huskiness. He shivered, coughed as he reached for the bottle again.

"Baby, huh?" he retorted huskily. "Kid, when you were blatting like a stinking sheep for the pap in your bottle, I was carrying whiskey like a man. But when I wake up an' see a ghost at my door, it's time to taper off."

He put down the second drink as another man chuckled, "You right sure, Doc, it wasn't a pink rattler at your door?"

Doc Middleton shuddered as he poured a third drink. "I've treated plenty of pink snakes and green elephants in the last thirty-eight years, gentlemen. But when Henry Middleton sees the ghost of Long Tom Forbes at his office door. . . ."

Mort Hayden threw his cigar on the floor. "You're crazy, Doc. Tote that bottle back to bed. Tom Forbes was killed in a back room here months ago."

The medico turned from the empty glass, licking his lips, blinking as he nodded. "Don't I know it, Hayden? Didn't I pronounce Tom dead myself, from a bullet wound in the head, fired in self-defense by Yuma Miles? Didn't I watch while he was buried up there on the hill?" Doc Middleton shuddered, closed his eyes for a moment. His husky voice dropped to a mutter. "Tom Forbes at my office door like he was thirty years ago, when he was riding high with the San Rico. It's time for Henry Middleton to swear off."

The Arizona Kid grinned again as Doc Middleton reached for the bottle. "Thirty years is a hell of a ways to go back for a ghost, Doc."

"They never die," Doc Middleton mumbled thickly. "They come looking for the men who lied about them. They come hunting the men who murdered them."

"Stop that drunken mumbling!" Mort Hayden rasped angrily. "Take the bottle and get out!"

Doc Middleton spoke thickly to the bottle. "Can't run away from ghosts. We was young an' San Rico was young. Tom, you've got young again . . . an' I'm an old booze hound who ain't. . . ."

Mort Hayden ripped out an ugly oath as he started toward the half-dressed little medico. A man standing next to Hayden stopped him with a quick hand on his arm. Hayden saw the stranger coming in from outside and turned to stare.

Doc Middleton looked around, still mumbling, and froze, eyes fixed on the door. Even Four Bits, the fat bartender, became a part of the quick, wary grimness that fell over the room as the stranger walked to the bar.

Trail dusty and needing a shave, the newcomer was built on the short side, wiry and smoothly deliberate in his movements. His smile broadened as he shoved back a dusty hat and spoke easily. "'Morning, everybody. Ain't that short-cut trail over from Bear Spring hell?"

Mort Hayden's smooth pink face had gone expressionless—and that was never a good sign with Mort Hayden. "You from Bear Spring, mister?"

"Whiskey," ordered the stranger amiably across the bar. He ignored Hayden's stare at dried blood on a torn coat sleeve and reached for tobacco and paper as he nodded. "I came through Bear Spring. Almost lost my horse before dawn on that big slide this side the top of the trail. He got panicky when the rotten rock slid under him. He was kicking over the drop before I got him stopped."

"That where you hurt your arm?" asked Hayden.

"A sharp rock gashed into it." The stranger nodded.

"Hurryin', wasn't you?" Mort Hayden asked with the same expressionless face. "That old back trail calls for daylight travel."

Sleep and fatigue had left the stranger's eyes bloodshot and marked the weathered skin under a blond stubble of beard. He nodded again as he lifted the drink. "Nobody told me how bad it was. The spring water up there tasted good, but this'll taste better." He drank, smacked his lips, nodded. "It does." He glanced at Doc Middleton's sagging face, at the shaved freshness of Mort Hayden, at the others standing there. Lighting the cigarette he had built, he smiled easily at them all.

"I'm looking for Jim Short. Anybody got an idea where I can find him?"

Silence followed that—a flat, grim silence that stretched out.

Mort Hayden's face remained without expression. "Jim Short a friend of yours?"

"Never saw him."

"Hayden's my name. I own the bar here."

"Howdy," the stranger said amiably. "I'm called Denver. About Jim Short now . . . ?"

Mort Hayden suddenly smiled crookedly. "My guess is

that Short's anywhere from here to hell an' gone. Maybe you'll find him hanging around that old cabin in Water Cañon where he's been staying. A mile north of town and turn to your right up the cañon. Look for a big cottonwood. The cabin's on the right."

"Thanks."

Denver paid for his drink and walked out. As the swinging doors closed behind him, Mort Hayden stopped smiling and scowled at Doc Middleton.

"Is that your blasted ghost, Doc?"

The medico drew a jerky breath, nodded sheepishly as he turned back to the bottle.

"Guess he is. I . . . I must have had a nightmare. He don't look like he did outside my office door. I could've sworn . . . ."

"You blatting old fool," Hayden snapped in a sudden return to ugliness. "Get out!" He snatched out a fresh cigar, bit off the end, scowled at the sound of the stranger riding away.

The Arizona Kid chuckled. "Ain't *he* gonna be surprised? I got a mind to follow an' watch him."

"Good idea," Hayden said abruptly. "Don't let him see you. There's an old path over into the cañon from the other side of the San Rico dump."

Grinning, the Arizona Kid nodded. "I've used it. Gimme a drink quick, Four Bits, while he gets out o' sight. Hey, Doc, watch them ghosts."

Doc Middleton had hitched up the other side of his trousers, grabbed the bottle off the bar, and started back the way he had come. He slammed the passage door without answering.

Mort Hayden glowered after him. "Someday I'll run that old soak out of town," he said angrily. "Underfoot here all the time like a drunken hog, gobbling about the fine gentleman he was."

"And about that time"—the Arizona Kid grinned—"somebody'll have to get patched up quick an' you'll yell for the doc."

The man called Denver walked his drooping claybank horse along the rutted street and stared about. San Rico, the town was named—Saint Rich Man. And up there on the scarred side of the mountain were the rusty, rotting, tumbled-down buildings of the old San Rico Mine to prove it.

Two millions and better in high-grade silver, by smelter records, had come out of the San Rico. Close to another million had come out of the smaller mines around about. But all that was in the past, back there in the years before the San Rico values had played out, before silver had dropped, and most of the smaller mines had closed. Since then fire had gutted and devoured San Rico. Storms and rot had added havoc to the flimsy shacks and crude cabins where miners, dance-hall girls, prospectors, and motley mining town followers had lived fast, wildly—and left hastily. Brush grew over the gopher holes on the mountain slopes. One person lived in San Rico where ten had lived before.

But there was cattle country in the lowlands to the west. Along the rutted, dusty main street came the stage road, dropping down from the southern shoulder of the mountain, looping, descending to the west toward Sand City and the railroad. A little ore still went out of the district. There was some trading from the ranch country. San Rico had more life than one would have suspected. Some of that the stranger knew, some he guessed now as he walked the claybank along the main street.

He'd not been blind to the wary grimness when he entered the saloon. Now he noted men breaking off low-voiced conversations to stare as he rode past. Something was in the air. Jim Short would know—not that it mattered much.

Denver was yawning when he reached the small cañon just north of town and turned up the trail. Grass crowded over the old wagon ruts, brush reached in from the sides. A little mountain stream roiled on the left. The sun was reaching into the morning chill of the cañon shadows when Denver sighted a big cottonwood ahead and a cabin roof off to the right. Then he saw something else.

The man called Hayden had told the truth. Jim Short was here. He was hanging around his cabin this morning. He was hanging from the bottom branch of a great cottonwood, stiffly, gruesomely hanging by his neck, with his hands tied behind and a red bandanna hiding his face.

II

An old one-horse wagon had been backed under the body. The horse was plunging, snorting nervously at such close contact with death. A boy holding the horse's head was shrilly calling: "Stand still, durn you, Ned! Whoa there! I'll bust your hard head wide open!"

A girl, trying to keep her balance on the lurching wagon bed, staggered, caught the sideboard to steady herself as Denver covered the intervening space at a quick gallop.

She was pale, eyes tear-wet. She was poignantly slender and young as she held a knife with which she had been about to cut down the body. Her look blazed at Denver in scornful anger as he came up.

"Keep away from us!" she warned. "I'll do this if every coward in San Rico tries to stop me!"

She snatched up an old carbine that had been lying on the wagon bed.

"Cowards!" she gulped as Denver dismounted. "All of you! Lying, skulking, hanging a man in the night when you caught him helpless! Haven't you done enough, without wanting him to h-hang here?"

She was close to weeping; her finger was convulsive on the trigger. Denver studied her.

"Don't start nothin' with Abby!" The boy's voice trembled with shrill warning. "I'll come a-slashin' when she shoots you!"

He was all of twelve, wearing patched overalls and a faded hickory shirt. He had released the bridle, whipped out a battered Barlow knife. His thin body was tensed to rush.

Denver smiled bleakly and lifted his arms.

"Can't argue with a gun and a knife. Lady, pull those sights a little to one side, please."

He moved back a step. The wagon horse took that moment to jump nervously, rear around, snorting. The girl's rifle crashed as she lost her balance and tripped over the wagon side.

The bullet burned Denver's side as he jumped forward to catch her. She fell heavily into his arms. The rifle clattered on the ground beside them. For a moment the girl was light in Denver's arms, fragrantly sweet, startled, and helpless against his body.

"Git your dirty hands off her!"

The boy was coming furiously at them with the Barlow knife. The girl caught her breath with a gasp and pushed away as Denver lowered her to the ground.

"That make it all right, son?" Denver inquired gravely.

The boy stopped uncertainly, glowering as he held the knife ready. "Don't call me son, durn you," he said resentfully.

"Jig, be careful!" the girl said hastily.

"I ain't the one to be careful. I'm a-watchin' him."

"And doing a good job of it," Denver said gravely. He put a finger in the lead-torn hole through the side of his coat. "Close-shooting, ma'am. You mighty near got me."

She was visibly dismayed now at her nearness to killing a man. The wagon wheels cramped sharply as the horse lunged away.

"Stop him, Jig!" she cried.

The boy wavered, then darted after the wagon that was careening up the cañon through weeds and brush.

"Whoa, Ned, durn you! Whoa! I'll yank your hammer head clean off! Whoa, you Ned!"

"Want me to help?" Denver asked the girl.

"Jig will do it," she replied stiffly.

Denver handed the carbine back to her. "Next time, ma'am, get on the ground before you throw your sights on a man. Killing by accident comes harder than cold-blooded shooting."

She flushed at his dry smile, but her reply was tight with challenge. "I'll not be stopped in this. Jim Short was our friend. I . . . I. . . ." She glanced at the dangling body, looked away, chin trembling.

Denver's smile vanished as he looked at the body.

"They call me Denver," he said quietly. "I rode into town this morning to see Jim Short. Let me get him down."

She stood wordlessly while he swung into the saddle again, and rode over beside the body. He cut the hang rope,

and turned the horse toward the cabin with the body in his
arms.

It was not a pleasant business, nor easy, getting Jim Short
down to the curly grass there before the cabin. Breathing
hard from the effort, Denver entered the cabin, came out a
moment later with a blanket that he threw over the body.

The girl had followed with the rifle and stood watching.
They could hear Jig's shrill, scolding voice up the cañon,
the *crackle* of undergrowth as the wagon turned. A jay called
harshly back in the trees. The girl's enmity and challenge
had ebbed away.

"I'm Abby McKnight," she said in a low voice. "That
was my brother Jig."

Denver removed his hat. "Glad to know you, ma'am . . .
even at a time like this." His face hardened. "Who did it?"

Her gesture was helpless. "Jig went to the store this
morning and heard. It . . . it happened sometime last night.
Jig says no one admits knowing who did it. Jim had been accused of a killing. There was talk against him, even though
Jig and I were able to swear he couldn't have done it."

Frowning, Denver asked: "Jim Short killed a man?"

"They said he did," Abby McKnight replied. "It was a
sneaking no-account called Big-Ear Berry. He was worth-
less and shiftless and always seemed to be slipping around
listening to what people were saying. But after he was dead
no one talked of that."

Denver nodded. "How'd it happen?"

"He was found off the trail just this side of the old Silver
Girl Mine, which Jim was working," explained the girl. "He
must have sneaked there to see what Jim was doing. Brock
Burns, the deputy, arrested Jim for the killing."

"And you know it didn't happen that way?" Denver
asked keenly.

"The afternoon that Berry was killed, Jim Short was at our place and stayed for supper," Abby said. "It was dark when he left. Too dark to shoot a man hiding off the trail, even if Jim had walked on up to the mine, which he said he didn't do."

"You believed him, ma'am?"

"Of course," she said promptly. She glanced at the still form under the blanket and swallowed. "Jim was that kind of a man," she said softly. "You believed him. In Sand City the day before yesterday, Jig and I told Judge Hardesty how Jim had spent the day repairing our cabin roof and hadn't gone near his mine. Judge Hardesty believed us. He let Jim come home until the trial. He said Jim would have to stand trial, but he'd probably get off. There wasn't any real proof that he killed Berry."

"So he got hung instead," Denver said under his breath.

Abby nodded sadly. "Jig heard that Mort Hayden said to let the body hang until the law took it down. Brock Burns, the deputy, is in Sand City. I. . . . I couldn't let Jim hang here."

Denver slowly rolled a cigarette. Jig was bringing the wagon back. His shrill voice floated through the shady quiet.

"Jim Short wasn't liked, ma'am?" Denver asked.

"Mort Hayden didn't like him. Our father was killed by a rock fall in the San Rico, which he had leased. Hayden wanted to buy the lease from me. Jim said not to sell. Hayden insisted that Jim was giving me bad advice."

Denver looked at her curiously. "You hold the lease on that old San Rico Mine, ma'am?"

She nodded.

"Funny anyone would want to lease it," Denver commented.

"My father, Tim McKnight, was shaft boss of the old San Rico, before the high-grade faulted out," Abby told him. "When the San Rico closed, he left like everyone else. But he always had an idea the high-grade could be found again. Four years ago, after mother died, Father wrote Mister Forbes, who owned the San Rico, and leased the mine on shares."

"Plenty of men have gone broke trying that sort of thing," Denver commented laconically.

"Father knew the San Rico like the back of his hand," Abby McKnight said with a quiet pride. "He could get out enough ore to live on while he tried to trace that faulted high-grade."

"Seems to me I've heard," remarked Denver, "that the San Rico owners spent almost a quarter of a million before they gave up trying to find that lost high-grade."

"Father would have found it," she said with the same quiet confidence.

Jig stopped the wagon down the slope and called: "We gonna take him to the buryin' ground?"

"The law has to look around first," Denver replied.

"Darn the law! It ain't none of Brock Burns's business!"

"I've got to sleep," Denver told Abby McKnight. "Might as well catch a wink here. Can you get a coffin and see about the grave? After the law has its say, we'll bury him."

"Sleep here?" she said uncertainly.

"I've been riding all night, ma'am. I'll pay for the coffin. Any amount."

"Please . . . we want to."

Denver nodded understandingly. "You might let folks know I'm watching the body and waiting for the law."

"You knew him?" she asked, still uncertain. "Were you his friend?"

"I never saw him before," Denver told her calmly. "I was just stopping by to talk with him."

She looked disappointed, but said nothing. Denver suddenly lowered his voice. "Somebody's watching us. Don't show that I'm saying anything much. Who would a little fat man be in San Rico? Gray mustache and a hard drinker by his looks."

Abby McKnight gave him a quick, searching look. Her voice instinctively dropped, too. "That sounds like Doc Middleton. Is . . . is *he* watching us?"

"No, he ain't the one." Denver indicated his torn coat sleeve and smiled ruefully. "I fell off my horse last night an' cut my arm. If you get a chance, tell the doc I'm going to need patching up a little."

Abby nodded, and left him there. As she drove away, Denver unsaddled the claybank and turned him to grass and water.

Denver's eyes were hard as he carried his saddle into the cabin and looked about the dim interior. There was the bunk from which he had taken the blanket, a stove, table, two chairs, cloths on nails driven into the logs. A shelf beside the stove held canned goods, and on another small shelf books were neatly arranged. A miner's candlestick was driven into the wall, an axe leaned inside the door. You could almost believe that Jim Short lingered here among his meager possessions. But Jim Short would not have thrown several of those books roughly onto the floor.

Denver stepped to the side window and eyed the undergrowth behind the cabin. Abby McKnight's wagon had passed from hearing. The jays were screaming again, and a moment later branches back in the undergrowth moved slightly and a head lifted into view.

Denver had marked a slight movement there as he had

talked with the girl. Now his eyes narrowed as he recognized the bony, intent face of the Arizona Kid, who had been in the San Rico Bar. After a minute or two the Kid turned noiselessly away in the undergrowth. Denver left his post at the window.

The table held a bucket of water and soap. Towels and a tin basin hung on a nail above. Denver stripped to the waist, washed, shaved with a razor that he took from his pocket, unwrapped the bloody bandage on his arm, and inspected the wound.

The ragged tear in coat and shirt sleeve might have been made by a sharp rock corner—or a finger. The hole in the arm muscles had undoubtedly been made by a bullet. Bleeding had stopped; infection was not yet feverish. Denver found a clean shirt belonging to the dead man, tore it up, bandaged the arm again. Then he took a look around the cabin.

New iron brackets had been fastened to the door sides. A new wooden bar leaned in the corner.

"Looking for trouble, were you?" Denver muttered as he barred the door.

He spread the remaining blanket on the bunk, put his gun under his pillow, and was asleep a few moments after he stretched out.

It seemed short minutes later that loud hammering on the door brought him rolling off the bunk into a crouch. His hand scooped the six-gun from under the pillow, his eyes blinked away the last fog of sleep.

The bony, grinning face of the Arizona Kid ducked away from the window.

III

Someone hammered on the door again. It sounded as though a gun butt were being used.

"Wake up in there!" a voice called impatiently.

"Coming," Denver answered.

Judging by the sun, it was well past noon. Denver reckoned that there were at least two men out there. He set the door bar quietly in the corner, thumbed back the gun hammer, stepped quickly aside as he opened the door.

"You must be lookin' for trouble!" was the greeting he received.

The speaker had just holstered a gun. Thumbs hooked in the belt, he stared suspiciously under a down-pulled hat brim. He was a big man, muscular, with a reddish mustache and wide, heavy lips that were smiling with half a sneer.

Denver uncocked the gun, looked past the big man at the Arizona Kid and two others.

"Might have been another hanging party for all I knew," Denver said calmly.

"You done anything to git hung for, stranger?" he was challenged.

"Depends on how bad you want another hanging," retorted Denver. He nodded at the body. "Did *he* do anything to get hung for?"

The big man reddened. "I don't want a hanging any time. I'm Brock Burns, the deputy. Just come from Sand City an' heard there'd been trouble here."

"Jim Short would have called it trouble, anyway," Denver agreed, stepping out. "Too bad you happened to be away last night. I'm called Denver. There's the body. The rope's still on the tree."

"Denver what?"

"Denver Colorado, if it sounds any better."

The Arizona Kid guffawed. "Burns, you learnin' your geography?"

The deputy reddened. "Where you from?" he snapped at Denver. "How come you're here today usin' Short's cabin?"

"I rode over from Bear Spring last night," Denver explained. "And stayed here with the body until the law showed up . . . from wherever it had left for last night."

"I don't like the sound of that," Burns said angrily.

"It did sound funny that you lit out that way," Denver agreed with a straight face. "But that's for local folks to talk about. I'm only a stranger who cut down the body for you and got some sleep while waiting for you to show up. Any objections?"

The Arizona Kid chuckled. "Burns, you're lookin' more like a skunk every minute. Better stop talking."

Burns was red and furious. "I came here to see about the hanging."

"Denver Colorado there," said the Arizona Kid, grinning, "wasn't around last night. I seen him reach town this mornin'. Doc Middleton says the hangin' was by parties unknown. Ain't much else to do but ride back for a drink, is there?"

"I want to know about this man," Burns said heavily. "What's his business here?"

"I stopped to see Short about a mine he was interested in," Denver stated.

"That old Silver Girl tunnel that Short was peckin' away in?"

"Is that the name of his mine?"

"You don't know nothin', do you?"

Denver looked at Jim Short's stiffening body that they

had uncovered. "I know Short was hanged. Do you know any more?"

"No," Burns said angrily. "Are you takin' charge of the body?"

"If the law is through with him."

"It shore as hell is. An' I'll tell you what oughta been told Short. Don't get hasty with your gun around here."

"Plain enough." Denver nodded. "You'll find me stepping wide from trouble . . . if trouble lets me alone."

Burns growled something under his breath and walked toward the saddled horses.

The Arizona Kid lingered, the reckless grin still on his bony face. "It ain't that we don't like strangers, Colorado. But a hangin' in San Rico shames us. We like the man to stay hung . . . an' forgot."

"Speaking for yourself or somebody else?" Denver countered.

The Kid chuckled. His eyes had greenish depths in which the humor seemed to dance even more plainly than on his angular, ugly face. "I'll buy a drink when you come to town, Colorado. Kind o' tickled me to see Brock Burns tangled in his own rope. He ain't any too smart, but he won't believe it."

"Thanks for the friendly offer."

The Arizona Kid showed white teeth. "I ain't friendly with anyone. You tickled me . . . an' maybe I'm sorry for you. I'll buy a drink, anyway."

Denver took up the blanket and covered the body again as they rode off. He caught and saddled the claybank and waited for Abby McKnight. After a time when he heard the rattle of the approaching wagon, the shrill tones of the boy, Jig, he was conscious of quick relief that they'd had no trouble.

The wagon carried a fresh board coffin. Abby McKnight said simply: "We couldn't get anything better. I don't think Jim would mind."

"He'd rather have this from you than the best in Sand City," Denver guessed.

Her look was grateful. "We'll have to drive through town to the burying ground."

"Any reason why we shouldn't?"

She gave him a troubled glance. "Some people will be asking why you bother with this."

The mask of hardness settled on Denver's face, making bleak, lean angles. "I'm always willing to answer questions," he said evenly, and turned to the task of getting the body into the board coffin.

Jig vanished. When he came in sight again, he was furtively wiping eyes on the patched sleeve of his shirt.

"Like to ride my horse while I drive?" Denver asked him.

The youngster's face set stubbornly. "Abby 'n' I'll drive him."

Denver nodded.

They took Jim Short to the burying ground that way, in the plain board box, riding in the bumpy, creaky old wagon. Abby McKnight drove, sitting pale and erect on the wagon seat with Jig beside her. Denver sided them on the claybank.

San Rico had never had a simpler burial. There was nothing about the old wagon creaking through the dust to draw attention. But somehow, some way, San Rico was interested. Word had evidently spread that the hanged man would come through town.

Denver saw them waiting as the wagon came to town. Gun-hung men, booted miners, loitering on the walks, here and there a woman in a doorway.

Denver's inscrutable glance took them in. Some of the men must have helped hang Jim Short; others had stayed in San Rico and let the body hang as Mort Hayden had ordered.

Most of the women were young, bold-looking. A good many of the men were hard-faced, swaggering, looking as if they might be as alien to San Rico as Denver. One and all were silent—in the same grim way that silence had fallen when Denver entered Mort Hayden's saloon. It was the silence of men who closed their mouths and waited for the break of trouble.

A group straggled out of the San Rico Bar and waited for them to pass. Mort Hayden was among these, smoking a long thin cigar, which he took from his mouth as the wagon creaked slowly past. The sardonically grinning Arizona Kid was there, also.

Denver's look met Hayden's stare for a moment. The saloon owner gave no sign. And then the wagon was past, moving slowly up the grade toward the rough weedy burial ground.

As they passed through the sagging picket fence into the cemetery, Denver looked back, to see who was following to watch the burial. There was no one.

Abby McKnight caught the look. Her voice was scornful, bitter. "They'll not cross Mort Hayden."

"A man," Denver told her, "with friends to bury him can do without the trimmings."

They reached the boothill of the old roaring San Rico. Uncut grass and weeds, rotting grave markers were forlorn inside the sagging fence. There were newer graves, too. And there was a wrinkled Indian in torn overalls and greasy old coat leaning on a shovel beside a newly dug grave.

"Charley Moose." Abby McKnight identified him for

Denver. "Jim treated him decently."

Charley Moose had brought two old ropes. It took the efforts of all of them to lower the heavy box into the grave. Charley Moose stood stolidly while Denver muttered a brief prayer. Abby McKnight was wiping her eyes when Denver helped her back on the wagon.

"I'll take you home, ma'am," he said quietly. "If there's anything else I can do, I'll be staying at Jim's cabin. It's as good a place as any."

"Don't," she warned hastily. "I was going to tell you. I was asked to tell you. Get out of San Rico today. You're not safe here."

"Who said so?"

"You'll have to take my word."

"Naturally." The stony look returned to Denver's face as he looked up at her. "I'm not safe . . . but you are. And this Mort Hayden wants your lease on the San Rico Mine. Are you sure you're safe?"

"Yes."

"You're trusting Hayden plenty," Denver said dryly. "I'll take a chance on him, too."

IV

San Rico began to stir as night closed over the decay and neglect. Windows showed lights; people appeared who had not been visible during the day. Scattered riders began to drift in. Twice groups of riders came fast and noisily out of the ranch country to the west. Music, laughter, and loud talk became audible in Mort Hayden's San Rico Bar.

Doc Middleton, still unshaved, unsteady from a long

sober day of worry and hard thought, stood in his small shabby office and gulped a drink he'd needed for hours. He almost dropped the glass when the door opened quietly and the man called Denver stepped in.

"You still around?" blurted the medico.

"Still around," Denver said briefly.

Doc Middleton put the glass on the worn oilcloth of the operating table and eyed his visitor with fascination.

"I cut my arm last night." Denver removed his coat, unwrapped the crude bandage, smiling grimly as Doc Middleton's bloodshot eyes looked up from the wound. "I've heard Tom Forbes say you beat anybody patching up people."

"Tom Forbes!"

"My uncle," Denver said. "Friends, weren't you?"

Doc Middleton swallowed and nodded.

"I was in the Argentine when Long Tom was killed," Denver continued. "Dealt extra aces, I heard, and was shot by a man named Yuma Miles."

Doc Middleton nodded again.

"Long Tom was handy with extra aces, wasn't he?"

The medico swallowed, reddened—and exploded. "No, by Satan! Long Tom Forbes never dealt a crooked card in his life. You're a hell of a nephew."

"I was wondering why no one nailed that story around here," Denver said calmly.

"Got me that time, didn't you?" Doc Middleton said huskily. "Go on. Tell me I'm a dirty skunk because I didn't do anything. They buried him and I kept my mouth shut."

"What happened?"

"Yuma Miles murdered Tom and had witnesses planted in the game to back him up," the doctor said heavily. "I wasn't in the room. I couldn't have proved they were lying. They'd have killed me if I'd tried."

"Who is this Yuma Miles?"

"A killer. A skunk. A curly wolf. Mort Hayden's personal gunman."

"Mort Hayden?" said Denver. "I wondered. What did Hayden have against Long Tom Forbes?"

"Nothing at first," Middleton said. "Long Tom come back here busted to see Tim McKnight, who had leased the San Rico. After Tim was killed, Tom stuck around. Said he'd made good here once and he had a hunch he'd do it again. The night he was killed, Tom was celebrating. When the liquor took hold, Tom threw some ore pieces on the bar an' boasted he'd take another fortune out of the San Rico." Doc Middleton's eyes gleamed at the memory. "Wire gold. High-grade. The San Rico never showed much gold value. But there it was . . . two or three thousand to a ton, if it ran a dime. Tim McKnight must have broke it just before a rock fall killed him. There isn't any doubt Long Tom was telling the truth. He was on a roaring drunk to celebrate."

"And he was roped into a poker game and Mort Hayden's man killed him?"

Doc Middleton nodded.

"Now Mort Hayden's trying to buy the San Rico lease from Miss McKnight," Denver murmured thoughtfully.

"After Long Tom Forbes was shot, no one ever found a trace of that high-grade," Doc Middleton said. "Maybe it'll never be found. The San Rico's a big mine. Without high-grade, the lease isn't worth much to Abby McKnight. Hayden says he's willing to gamble."

"Jim Short advised her not to sell the lease . . . and got charged with a killing and then hanged."

Doc Middleton nodded.

Denver eyed the dried blood on his arm. "This man Berry was shot after dark near Jim Short's mine. Maybe somebody thought he was killing Jim Short."

"I wondered about that," Doc Middleton confessed.

"The Sand City judge turned Jim Short loose . . . and Jim was hung. Now there's no one to hold Abby McKnight back from selling her lease."

"She can sell to Mort Hayden . . . or she can marry Mort Hayden," stated Doc Middleton huskily. "Mort'd rather have the last. It's cheaper and Abby's something different from his saloon girls. Hayden doesn't want any strangers around giving Abby more advice. He doesn't want anyone around who might remind him of Long Tom Forbes. I'll fix that arm. Run for it before the next bullet does better. You didn't get this one in San Rico," he remarked as he hurriedly went to work.

"I got it last night, this side of Bear Spring," Denver said. "Fellow who'd heard me asking directions caught up with me and said he was riding to San Rico, too. The moon had been up a couple of hours before he made his play. Almost got me, too. He had a letter with his name on it. Turk Anderson."

Doc Middleton started so violently he spilled water from the pan he was putting on to heat.

"Turk Anderson. Holy hell, you're already dead if the Arizona Kid, Bud Wise, or Johnny Gort hears it. They've been waiting for Turk to ride in."

"It's a waste of time."

Doc Middleton clattered the pan on the little heating stove and turned, face working. "You're ignorant, young man!" he raged. "Since Mort Hayden came here three years ago, San Rico has been buzzard's roost for wanted men. Brock Burns only thinks when Hayden says to. They spend their money here, rest up, outfit, and hide out in the old mines around here if outside law shows up. There's always gunmen to settle those who differ with Hayden's way." He reached for the whiskey bottle again. His voice was harsh with earnestness. "The ranchers are feeling it. Their hands stop in here, get drunk, fight, and gamble their money away. Sometimes they get killed. Gunmen who leave their money with Hayden rustle a little for a stake. The stage has been robbed twice in the last six months. The Arizona Kid and his friends are among the worst. When they find you killed Turk Anderson. . . ." He shook his head hopelessly as he put down the bottle.

Denver rolled a cigarette. "Thanks, Doc," he said quietly. "When I was a kid, Long Tom used to speak of San Rico. He always called you a square shooter. I knew about Hayden and San Rico before I started here. I had an idea this Turk Anderson had friends. I ran his horse off, hid his saddle, buried him a mile off the trail in a rock crevice, under half a wagon load of stones. My business here calls for San Rico cleaned up and orderly. You've given me an idea."

"You aren't drunk," said Doc Middleton harshly. "But you sound like it. Drunk or crazy."

"Crazy, maybe," Denver agreed, breaking into a smile. "I've showed you my hand because Long Tom called you his friend. Fix my arm and forget it."

"Young fool," Middleton snorted. He was glowering, muttering irritably under his breath as he worked on the arm.

When he was through and Denver was putting on his coat, the medico said brusquely: "Still set on being a fool?"

"Call it that."

Doc again snorted, rubbed a hand over his stubbled face, and the bloodshot eyes were suddenly suspiciously bright. His voice had a new huskiness not caused by whiskey. "I know I'm a busted-down old soak. Nobody's called me a

198

square shooter for years. I backed off from mixing in Long Tom's murder. You'll be killed if I know San Rico and Mort Hayden. I'm not sure why you're here, son . . . but if there's anything I can do, speak up."

"Thanks." Denver nodded. "One more question, Doc. How is Miss McKnight fixed for money?"

"Tim McKnight left her and the boy mighty little. It's gone," Doc Middleton said heavily. "Abby's hung on, hoping to find that high-grade in the San Rico. Jim Short got her to take a little from him by swearing he'd like to gamble she'd find that high-grade. Now. . . ." He shrugged.

"And no work here," Denver guessed.

"She can marry Mort Hayden or turn saloon girl."

"I've got Hayden in mind," Denver said. From a money belt under his shirt he took some $20 gold pieces.

"She won't take it. She's proud," Middleton warned.

"Tell her Jim Short left it for her in case anything happened to him."

"It might. . . ." Doc Middleton left the sentence unfinished, darted to the back door, turned a key that had the door locked, and jerked the door open. "There he goes!" he exclaimed.

Denver reached him and heard running steps retreating.

"I heard that loose board on the back stoop creak," Doc jerked out huskily. "Couldn't see who he was. Better get out of town fast, young fellow. Can't tell what he heard."

A ragged burst of shots down the street held them both startled, inquiring.

"Mort Hayden's place!" Doc Middleton blurted.

Denver wheeled quickly to leave the office.

"Don't be fool enough to go there," the medico warned.

"I was going, anyway," Denver told him. "This may be just what I need."

V

The San Rico Bar was in an uproar. A tanned young cowman lay gasping on the floor. Bloody froth stained his mouth redder than the painted lips of the kneeling girl who held his head.

Chairs had been overturned. A roulette table at the back of the room was deserted. Customers, percentage girls stood uncertainly along the bar and opposite wall.

A long lanky cowman with a weathered hat back awry on his head was holding a bloody hand and speaking furiously to Mort Hayden.

"It was murder, damn you! Chris was drunk an' couldn't 'a' held a gun steady if he was minded to!"

Mort Hayden stood behind the bar chewing a long thin cigar and holding a sawed-off shotgun.

"Your man started it, Johnson," he said tightly. "I saw him go first for a gun. Yuma had to shoot in self-defense. If you hadn't jumped in to help, you wouldn't have been hurt."

Doc Middleton burst through the swinging doors carrying his worn old doctor's bag.

"How many?" he asked. "Two? One holed in the chest? Get his head up in your lap, Rose. Stop that damn' sniffling! The rest of you get back. Johnson, wrap a handkerchief around that wrist until I can get to you!"

Shabby, unshaven, nondescript, and dissipated, Doc Middleton had now a fire of authority that sent onlookers shuffling back from the body.

The crowd had divided, Denver noted. Seven men, looking like cowmen, mostly young, clean-looking, and range-toughened, had gathered behind the lanky Johnson. Beyond them was twice their number of hard-looking men, some sullen, some impassive, all wary for trouble.

Beyond the man on the floor stood the killer holding a cocked six-gun. You knew at the first look he was the killer. It wasn't the dried parchment-like skin over prominent face bones, the hooked nose, the pale lips, or the wary looseness of long legs ready for any move. The hollow burning eyes told you, eyes sneering at the dying man on the floor, at the lanky, raging Johnson, and the angry uncertain cowmen.

A sardonic voice spoke at Denver's elbow. "Maybe that drink'll do handy now, Colorado."

The Arizona Kid's bony face was grinning again. The Kid was unruffled, enjoying himself with the sardonic twist of humor that seemed to direct all his actions.

A quick look satisfied Denver that the Arizona Kid had no suspicion of what had happened to Turk Anderson.

"What's been going on here?" Denver inquired.

"Yuma slapped that gal, Rose. The cowboy had took a fancy to her an' was drunk enough to make it a quarrel."

The girl was sobbing quietly as she sat there on the dirty floor in a blue, low-necked silk dress and held the dying man's head. He was breathing harder, gasping, choking on the bloody froth rising into his throat.

Yuma spoke roughly to her: "Cut that squallin', Rose."

She threw him a frightened look, bit hard on her underlip to keep back the sobs. The hard, bleak angles came back on Denver's face as he watched. This was what a dance-hall girl in Mort Hayden's place could expect. Abby McKnight would have her share of it if she had to work for Mort Hayden.

"Who's the one with the shot-up hand?" Denver asked under his breath.

"Ramrod for the Cross T. I hear Old Man Higgins, the boss, has been raisin' hell about his 'punchers ridin' over here to San Rico." The Arizona Kid chuckled. "This'll make him snort an' tear. Want that drink?"

"Whiskey," Denver accepted.

The heavy-faced bartender tore his attention away from the taut quiet while Doc Middleton worked swiftly and deftly. Bottle and glasses were shoved at them.

Denver lifted his drink. "Quick shooting, mister . . . for both of us."

"Bad shootin' to the other guy," the Arizona Kid added, grinning.

"Plenty of it," Denver agreed. He was smiling faintly as he drank.

Doc Middleton stood up, wiping his hands on a small towel he'd taken from the old bag. The wounded man on the floor was quiet, eyes closed now.

"Will he make it?" Johnson asked harshly.

Doc Middleton squinted at him in surprise. "Better come over to my office and get that hand fixed, Johnson. The boy here is dead."

Johnson looked stunned, so quickly, quietly had death come.

The sneer stayed on Yuma Miles's face. He stood waiting with gun drawn.

Mort Hayden spoke metallically from behind the bar. "It'll be a lesson to the next man who gets an idea he can run things around here. He's your man, Johnson. Take him with you. And curb those hotheads behind you. They'll suffer if they start anything."

That was easy to believe. The gun Hayden leveled across the bar held buckshot. Yuma Miles was ready to shoot. Six-guns waited on every side.

Johnson choked on rage that was all the more bitter because it was helpless.

"It was murder, Hayden. You got the kind of witnesses you need. That damn' deputy, Burns, won't lift a finger, but it was murder. This ain't the end of it. How much longer do you think folks'll stand for the kind of place you're runnin' here?"

"Get out!" Mort Hayden rasped. "I'll run my place here. You run things out on the range. You're welcome here as long as you stay peaceable. Don't whine about what happens when you start trouble. Now get going!"

The Arizona Kid's eyes had a mocking mirth in their greenish depths.

"There it is, Colorado. Take it or leave it. How do you like it?"

"I'll think it over," Denver said. "My treat. Whiskey again?"

"And bad shootin' again for the other fellow."

"Worried?"

"I play safe." The Arizona Kid grinned.

They drank, watched the Cross T men carry out the dead cowpuncher. Within seconds the tension had vanished. Talk burst out. Men surged back to the bar. A girl laughed shrilly. Mort Hayden put the shotgun back under the bar.

Yuma Miles said something to the girl, Rose, as she passed him. She flinched and hurried on, pale and unhappy.

The bleak angles stayed on Denver's face as Yuma Miles passed close to him with no more than a casual look. Others recognized him as the man who had helped bury Jim Short. They stared, then ignored him when no one else appeared interested.

But Doc Middleton had been right. Coming here was a fool trick. A man could seldom find such a collection of cut-throats and hardcase gunmen. The Arizona Kid alone would be trouble enough for any two men if he had an idea his friend Turk Anderson had been shot by the stranger.

"Going to be around here long?" Mort Hayden asked Denver colorlessly across the bar as he held a match to a cigar.

"I like the town," Denver said casually.

Mort Hayden puffed leisurely and nodded. "So do I. Sometimes I don't like some of the things that happen. . . ." He shrugged.

"When you don't," Denver finished for him, "you take a hand in it?"

Hayden's eyes were as colorless as his voice. He had a trick of staring without blinking. "You found your man and you buried him," he remarked. "Anything else on your mind?"

"I found him hanging around . . . like you said," Denver said evenly. "If you're asking whether I'm wondering who hung him and why, I'm not."

The colorless eyes surveyed him without a flicker.

Denver noticed Yuma Miles near him. Miles was standing loose-kneed, loose-armed, with the same slight sneering smile he'd given the dying Cross T man. You could make a good guess that Yuma Miles had been sneering the same way after he murdered old Tom Forbes. Denver's cheek muscles ridged.

"I'm not drunk, Hayden," he said. "Better make sure that damn' buzzard isn't circling me for trouble."

The Arizona Kid chuckled. "I still got the taste of Colorado's likker in my throat, Mort. It'd be terrible if Yuma made a mistake."

Hayden looked at the Kid in surprise. Then he nodded, answered smoothly: "No one's going to make trouble, Kid."

"I didn't think so."

"Mort! Feller to see you!" the big bartender called. Hayden left them and Yuma Miles turned away.

"Mort don't like you, Colorado," the Kid warned. "Better move on."

At the back of the bar Hayden was talking to a short, stoop-shouldered man with a ragged reddish mustache. Denver saw the gambler glance toward the front where he was standing. Then Hayden called Yuma Miles over to him.

"If I don't get a chance to say it again, thanks for the advice and the drink," Denver told the Arizona Kid.

"You leavin'?"

"*Adiós.*"

The sardonic smile came again on the Kid's young bony face. "You shore take advice fast, Colorado."

Denver started to back toward the swinging doors as Yuma Miles made for the front of the room with long loose strides. Hayden was hurrying forward behind the bar.

He'd stayed too long, Denver realized now. The man who had eavesdropped at Doc Middleton's back door had gotten to Mort Hayden. Seconds now would show how much he'd overheard.

The Arizona Kid had lost his smile. His glance darted swiftly around when he realized that Denver was backing from trouble. No one else seemed to have noticed. The rough crowd was noisily careless again.

"Turk Anderson's dead, Kid!" Yuma called over to the Arizona Kid. "Thet damn' stranger shot him last night!"

The shrill cry of an alarmed bar girl marked the amazingly swift draw of Yuma Miles. The spouting roar of the shot drove everyone scattering, ducking out of the way.

Denver had plenty of warning—and he learned what a fool chance a man took who waited. Lead seared his side as he weaved instinctively and followed with the spurting crash of his own six-gun.

Yuma Miles had shot faster than one would have thought possible, had almost dropped Denver before he got started.

Then Yuma flinched as lead nicked him somewhere. Not badly, though. He was still coming forward when the girl called Rose darted to him and dragged down his gun arm. His second shot blasted into the floor.

Denver stopped his own second shot as the slim whirling body of the girl hid Yuma Miles for an instant. His back hit the swinging doors. He dodged outside, conscious of the staring hate mask of the Arizona Kid accepting the blood feud between them. The Kid's hand was streaking to get in a shot.

Denver was vanishing outside when the Kid's lead hit one of the swinging doors. An instant later the thundering blast of the shotgun splintered, tore the closing doors with buckshot.

Horses at the hitch rack were milling, plunging in fright. One evidently struck by a buckshot pellet broke loose and plunged kicking across the street.

Denver bolted toward his own horse that he had left tied before the shabby little one-story building where Doc Middleton lived and had his office.

There wasn't any chance to find out what had happened to the girl who had saved him from Yuma Miles's lead. The saloon was in an uproar. They'd be coming fast as soon as they were certain he wasn't waiting outside the door.

The Cross T men ran out of Doc Middleton's as Denver raced toward the spot. Behind him a six-gun hammered shots.

"Doc!" Denver yelled.

The Cross T men were getting out of the way.

"So you went and done it?" Doc Middleton's husky voice called from the office doorway.

"Hayden seems to know everything we said!" Denver panted. "See you later!"

The claybank was rested, ready, trained, and willing. When Denver came down hard in the saddle, the horse was already in a furious run.

Futile shots reached after him. The deeper roar of the shotgun broke out. The claybank jumped, began to run madly as a spent buckshot struck him. They were yelling, shouting back at the San Rico Bar as Denver whirled the claybank off the main street and galloped out of town.

The lights dropped behind, the night closed around him, and he whirled the horse off the narrow wagon road into the brush and trees. He was well away from the road, walking the claybank, when the first rush of pursuit passed on the road.

Five or six men at least, Denver estimated. A few stragglers drummed after them. Denver dismounted and led the horse.

Twenty minutes later he reached the road to Sand City, north of town, got his bearings, and shortly rode into the clearing where Abby McKnight's small, white flower-bordered house stood.

"I got a gun on you! What you want?" Jig's defiant voice challenged from the darkness.

"It's Denver."

"Oh." The youngster's voice was sulky as he demanded again: "What you want? We heard a heap of shootin' in town."

Then his sister's voice: "Jig, did you take that gun out

207

there, after all? Bring it here. Who are you talking to?"

Denver walked the horse toward her. "It's Denver, ma'am. Anyone been here yet?"

"No," she replied uncertainly. Denver swung down before her and spoke rapidly.

"Chances are Mort Hayden will come to see you. He knows who I am."

A white dress made her look slim and wraith-like in the faint starlight. Her calm comforted him with the assurance that guns and death hadn't been here in the quiet night. Yuma Miles, Mort Hayden, and the Arizona Kid hadn't as yet become a part of the peaceful clearing.

"Who are you?" Abby asked.

"I'm Long Tom Forbe's nephew. His will left the San Rico Mine to me. I bought that old Silver Girl Mine that Jim Short was digging in."

"I'll be durned!" Jig said behind them.

"Jig, please!" Abby looked at Denver. "I . . . I don't believe I understand what it's all about."

"I haven't got time to explain, ma'am. But I'm here in San Rico to stay. Hayden knows it now, knows I own the San Rico. No telling what he'll do about you."

"Why should he do anything about me?"

"You're leasing the San Rico. Hayden will think you know more than you do. Better get some place where you'll be safe until we know how all this is going to turn out."

"But I don't know anything and I'm safe enough here. I'm not afraid of Hayden."

"You'd better be afraid," Denver warned. "There's no telling what Hayden will do."

"If you own the San Rico and its worth all this, why should you want me to keep my lease?" she countered shrewdly.

"Why?" Denver repeated. "Why . . . because that's what I want. And I don't want you staying here without help."

"I have Jig."

"That's foolish talk. Will you listen to reason?"

"I've listened to you. We'll stay here."

"You heard her!" Jig spoke ominously from behind him.

Baffled, Denver glowered, gave it up. "How can I get to the Cross T?" he asked.

She told him and he left her there, slim in the starlight. It was too late to get Doc Middleton to reason with her. Denver put the claybank into a run on the Sand City road with a helpless, angry feeling that he was doing the wrong thing—and yet not knowing what else he could do.

VI

Old Man Higgins of the Cross T was like a piece of old whang string—weathered and worked until he was leather and sinew. His drooping mustache was gray; his blue eyes had fire and temper. A stream of profanity erupted as he stamped back and forth under the low-beamed ceiling of the Cross T ranch house.

"So one of them dirty sidewinders kilt Chris Evans. I knowed it'd happen one day. I told them boys to stay away from that bunch of skunks. Johnson deserved gettin' his hand shot. I'll fire him soon as he rides in. I'll fire all them triflin' young wasters. Served 'em right if they'd all been kilt." Old Man Higgins swung around, gray mustache bristling, eyes snapping. "You rode out here to tell me about it. What'n hell was you doin' while my men was gettin' shot up?"

"Me?" asked Denver, lighting a cigarette. "I was watching. Nobody said your men needed a nurse."

"Who'n hell said ary Cross T man needed a nurse? Them boys is the finest bunch workin' for ary cowman in these parts. Ain't a one of 'em I ain't proud of. But they ain't skunks, they ain't killers, thieves, rustlers. They . . . they. . . ."

Denver's grin stopped the old man in mid-speech.

"What'd you say your name was?" Old Man Higgins demanded suspiciously.

"I didn't say. I'm called Denver Forbes. Long Tom Forbes was my uncle. Maybe you knew him."

"Knew him," snorted Old Man Higgins. "Too well. I knowed him in the old days when he was ridin' high on the San Rico. He was a poker-playin' fool who'd bluff the store teeth offen his grandma's gums. Sent me home busted many a night when he couldn't even show pairs." The oldster quieted. There was a reminiscent gleam in his eyes. "Sure, plenty of us knowed Long Tom. His loans put cattle on our grass again after the big drought cleaned us. They killed him there in San Rico just like they did Chris Evans. Some of us old-timers tried to do something about it. But the feller who shot Tom had proof that we couldn't have busted in court."

Denver nodded. "And there's witnesses this time that your man drew first."

Old Man Higgins muttered angrily under his breath.

"Long Tom left me the San Rico Mine," Denver stated casually. "High-grade has been found that'll make the mine pay again. But first I'll have to clean out Hayden and his buzzards. Hayden is trying to get the mine and run the show himself. It'll be a job to open the mine and go ahead with Hayden and those gunmen trying to block me."

210

"The sheriff'll help you."

"The sheriff's at Sand City. Hayden pretty much runs San Rico. He's smart enough to use the law himself all he can. This'd be a good time to clean San Rico out."

Old Man Higgins looked at him sharply, then shook his head. "That's a large order. Not much chance of it happening. Things has been peaceable too long on this range, son."

"I was afraid so. Have to tackle it myself, I guess. I rode out here on the chance you might see it my way, Mister Higgins."

"You'll get kilt fast and quick."

"I'll take a chance."

Higgins listened. There were running horses coming. They went outside to watch.

The Cross T men were returning. Old Man Higgins stalked back to the horse corral and met them. His blistering profanity lashed the sullen riders.

Johnson flared back angrily. "I went to bring the boys back. Wouldn't have been any trouble if there was any kind of law in San Rico. Gimme a dozen good men an' we'll put law there before daylight."

"No more of that talk," Higgins ordered irritably. "Things is bad enough now. Go get some sleep. Forbes, bunk in the house. We'll talk some more in the morning."

"I'll move on," Denver decided. "No use waiting."

"You left hell boiling back there in San Rico." Johnson gave him gruff warning. "Better ride the other way. They're lookin' for you."

"I judged so," Denver said dryly.

"An' you'll be fool enough to go back!" Old Man Higgins cussed testily. "Stop in the house for some coffee first. And the first one of you hellions who rides outside Cross T fence before I say so, stays fired this time. That's turkey talk."

In the house kitchen the old rancher started a fire in the stove, set coffee on to heat, and talked as he worked.

"Bad towns has been cleaned up by one man. Mostly he was death on the draw an' the law was behind him. He had a bad 'un or two to bluff or outshoot and what was left mostly was ready to fall in line. He had a body of decent citizens backing him up. San Rico's all bad."

"Not all bad."

"I seen that town start," Old Man Higgins snapped, "an' I seen her die. I seen this Hayden take 'er over. The place ain't a one-man job now. Go back there alone tonight and Hayden'll have your damn' mine quick an' easy."

"Someone else maybe. Hayden won't."

"So you'll get Hayden at least?" Old Man Higgins commented sarcastically. "And you'll be dead and somebody else'll have the mine and the town. Are all you young folks fools? Do you have to be old, worn-out, busted down, and useless like me before you reason right? What's that?"

Someone had plunged into the front part of the house, bumping a chair as he cried in a strangled voice: "Mister Denver! Mister Denver!"

Denver beat his companion into the low-beamed front room. Jig McKnight was there, weaving, gasping for breath.

"They got Abby!" he choked. "You s-said you was comin' here! Our old hoss give out back there. I h-had to run the rest of the way!"

Jig's cheek was gashed, shirt torn half off. An eye was swollen and tears had furrowed grime on his cheeks. Small, despairing, and desperate, he stood there snuffling as Old Man Higgins snapped: "Who is he?"

"Name's McKnight. He and his sister live in San Rico.

212

Sit down, Jig. Was it Mort Hayden?"

Jig nodded as he sat on a chair edge.

"Doc Middleton came and was tellin' us to leave when Mort Hayden an' two other men walked in. Hayden c-cussed Doc for bein' there an' told him to get out. Doc said he was stayin' with us. Mort Hayden drew a gun. Doc called him a yeller dog not fitten to be with decent folks. An' . . . an' Mort Hayden said . . . 'You old fool. I'll teach you some sense.' . . . an' hit him with the gun. An' then he told Abby he come to get that mine lease settled. But Abby told him he'd never get it from her after hittin' Doc that way. And he grabbed her arm. An' . . . an' one of the fellers hit me clean acrost the room, so hard I didn't know what happened after that."

"Why did he hit you?"

"He was afeerd I'd shoot him with the rifle I grabbed up." Jig snuffled.

Old Man Higgins was swearing under his breath as Denver demanded: "What did Hayden do to your sister?"

"I don't know!" Jig wailed. "When I knowed anything next, there was only one feller left cussin' Doc. He went to the door an' I run out the back way. He come yellin' for me to stop but I got back of the shed in the trees. Our old hoss was hobbled in the grass down the road. I snuck the bridle out o' the shed an' rode here where you said you was comin'. I'm afeerd for Abby."

Denver put a hand on the boy's thin shoulder. "I'm going after her, Jig. She'll be all right."

"She better be all right," Old Man Higgins said ominously. "She better be smilin' an' safe when we get there. Nary a hair ruffled or harmed."

"We?" Denver queried.

"You heard me!" Old Man Higgins exploded. "We, I

said! I knowed Tim McKnight. Doc Middleton's done our work since he come out here a young man. Them snakes in San Rico has made one play too many. A woman. A mite of a helpless gal. And an old doctor that never done ary thing but help folks. We ain't got soft enough to put up with stuff like that. I'll git fifty men by tomorrow to clean out that place for good an' all."

"What about Abby McKnight and Doc Middleton while you're getting them?" Denver asked quietly.

Old Man Higgins's gray mustache was jerking with anger as he gestured helplessly.

"Come when you get ready," Denver told him, starting out of the room.

He was swinging on the claybank when he heard Old Man Higgins's harsh voice out back of the house:

"Crawl outta them bunks! Get your hosses saddled! Johnson! Sim! Clayhorn!"

VII

Denver rode under the bright stars in a sort of cold frenzy. Now he could see that something like this was bound to happen. He should have anticipated it. Abby McKnight hadn't had a chance since that night when Long Tom Forbes had showed high-grade gold and boasted of another fortune waiting for the taking. Long Tom had been killed. Jim Short had been killed. The stranger called Denver had been Abby's last hope. Denver groaned at his folly in leaving her while he went about his own business. He had an icy, helpless feeling that it was too late now to help her. Hayden was desperate, cold-blooded, knowing he had to work fast to cover his tracks. And Abby was stubborn. Brave and stubborn.

Denver reached the clearing where her small cabin stood and rode in with gun drawn. No voice or gun challenged him. A lamp still burned in the cabin. He looked through a window, swore softly at sight of a dead man on the floor. Not Doc Middleton. This bearded dead man had been in the San Rico Bar with Mort Hayden early this morning.

Only this morning! It was hard to believe that in a single day life could turn so bloody and desperate. Even when you knew all about San Rico and had arrived ready for trouble. Hard to believe, too, that Doc Middleton could have killed that bearded gunman. But Jig had said the Doc was held by Hayden's man. There was Hayden's man—and Doc was gone.

The faint rattle of gunfire drifted on the sharp night wind from San Rico. A moment later Denver was riding toward the sound.

That wasn't a saloon brawl, flaring in a burst of shots and ending. The gunfire kept up. Denver was puzzled, expecting anything as he reached the first town shacks with cocked rifle across his saddle and belt gun loose in the holster.

The shooting was at the other end of town. Denver rode off the main street, skirted the shacks and cabins that time and fire had not destroyed. Among the scattered, intermittent shots he heard an occasional whoop and shout of laughter. He was still puzzled as he tied the claybank up the mountain slope near the old San Rico Mine and went down the slope with long strides.

A bullet shrilled through the starlight. Another whined, passing off to the left. Two sagging walls of an old ruined cabin loomed ahead. Beyond, down the slope, a muzzle flash licked red in the starlight. The scream of the bullet was close this time.

A rifle barked sharply behind one of the cabin walls. An amused voice shouted: "Pour it on, Doc! You got us bluffed!"

The gun down the slope flashed quickly again. Denver was close enough to hear the dull *thud* of the bullet on the logs.

"The old hellion's shootin' close!" a second voice said. "Damned if I ever thought he'd turn into a wildcat like this. An' that old, flea-bitten Injun, too. Ain't no wonder Mort said to lay 'em both out cold this time."

"Injuns is tricky. Watch for this 'n' to make a snake dash for the brush soon as their cartridges start to give out."

The speakers fired again. Denver could make out the cabin 100 yards down the slope where Doc Middleton must be. The San Rico main street was beyond the cabin. Doc and his companion were cornered. Denver had marked guns firing from all sides of the cabin. Now he stopped at the back of the single side wall and casually asked: "Where's Mort?"

They jumped. One of them swore. "Don't ease up on a body like that! Might've took you for that damn' Injun down there! Mort's in his house or the saloon, I guess. Who are you?"

"Johnny Gort," Denver said, naming one of the Arizona Kid's friends that Doc Middleton had mentioned.

A gun belched fire in answer. The bullet glanced from the end of a log and raked like a red branding iron through Denver's shoulder muscles as his cocked six-gun roared back. He dropped in a crouch, half sheltered by the old logs, and triggered the six-gun in a blazing roll of shots at their gun flashes and shadowy figures.

Log splinters showered his face. His hat jerked as the crown was holed. One man went down. The other bolted out into the open, quartering down the slope, shouting: " 'Nother one of 'em up here! Get him!"

Denver jumped to the wounded man in time to stamp a hand that was lifting a six-gun for another shot at him.

"Why shoot when I say Johnny Gort?" Denver demanded harshly.

"That damn' Injun down there shot Johnny Gort half an hour ago," the wounded man gasped.

"How come?"

"Doc Middleton snuck up behind Mort Hayden's house. Johnny seen him and jerked a gun an' didn't spot the Injun offside until it was too late. I know you now. You're the feller who helped bury that Jim Short. You holed me center. They'll get you. They're comin' for you."

"Where's Mort Hayden's house?"

"White house near the saloon. I. . . ."

Denver missed the rest. The run he made from the old cabin took him quartering down the slope the opposite way from the other man.

Anyone with sense would head back up the mountain and vanish in the brush, but maybe they wouldn't be looking for him to come down this way. The bleeding shoulder was hurting and the fire of his anger was blazing under his quick calculations.

Abby McKnight must be in Mort Hayden's white house near the saloon. Denver remembered the house, new, painted white, with a broad front porch. Who would have thought Doc Middleton had nerve enough to come back into town and try to enter that house? Or take to cover and fight back grimly, desperately. It reminded Denver of Old Man Higgins and other old-timers he'd known. They lived peaceably, put up with a lot for peace. But prod them too far, and no gunman on the owlhoot was more reckless and deadly.

Old Man Higgins had been right. One man or two didn't have much chance against this bunch in San Rico.

Men were rushing the old cabin back up the slope. Denver dropped behind a bush as running steps circled to his right. The man went on without seeing him. Denver skirted a cabin, an old deserted store building, and came out on the shadowy main street.

Not everyone had been shooting at Doc Middleton and the Indian. Horses were hitched along the street; indistinct figures were out in the open, standing in doorways. Lights were bright in the San Rico Bar, as if nothing was happening.

Denver cut across the street at a slower walk, skirted to the back of another building, hurried behind Mort Hayden's saloon toward the new white house. Remembering that Doc Middleton and the Indian had met someone watching back of Hayden's house, he hugged the shadows, watched the night ahead as he came to the rear of the white house.

A sarcastic chuckle from the shadows back of the porch met him: "That you, Colorado?"

Denver dived to the ground as a shotgun thundered from the shadows. The scatter charge ripped the crown out of his hat, raked and tore his scalp with odd pellets, and slammed him, bleeding, stunned, on the ground. He heard the Arizona Kid chuckle again.

"I thought you'd foller the doc an' come lookin' for her, Colorado. You drank to quick shootin', an' you got it. Turk Anderson'll shore laugh when he sees your face full of scatter shot."

The back door of the house jerked open as the Arizona Kid came out of the shadows.

"Your man come, Kid?"

"Got him right in the face. He never moved," the Kid chuckled.

"No, you don't! Stand still!" the man in the house violently ordered someone inside.

The Arizona, Kid laughed again. "Better make Mort look after his own women. Both of you, Yuma, pick the damnedest wildcats."

"If she was mine, I'd cripple her like I did Rose," Yuma Miles snarled, and slammed the door.

Blood was running in Denver's eyes, hammers seemed to be beating inside his skull as he fought the pain, the dizziness and weakness, and tried to lift the sudden great weight of the six-shooter that he still clutched.

This was death. The Arizona Kid looming out of the shadows was death. He'd shoot fast again at the first sign of life here on the ground.

The Kid was close when Denver gritted his teeth, rolled over, and started shooting. He heard the Kid yell. The shotgun roared again. The charge struck the ground at one side, and the Kid's sprawling fall dropped the smoking shotgun hard on Denver's shin.

The painful blow helped clear Denver's head. He heard himself muttering as he staggered up. "You didn't drink enough to bad shooting for the other fellow, Kid."

He'd dropped his gun but wasn't too dazed to look for it. The Kid was motionless. Denver clawed the Kid's six-gun from the holster as the house door jerked open again and Yuma Miles called: "What'n hell happened now?"

Yuma's eyes were full of the light inside. He didn't see the bloody, reeling figure that rose up out of the night and made for the back steps. But he heard the movement and stepped out on the back porch.

"Did you get another, Kid?" Yuma demanded harshly. Hand on gun, he peered out.

"Here's for Long Tom Forbes," Denver croaked, reeling up the steps.

Yuma Miles yelled with astonishment as the bloody face loomed in his vision—yelled and jerked his gun. Denver came at him half blinded with blood and hands mechanically triggering the two guns they gripped.

Yuma Miles was fast and rattled. He put a bullet in Denver's leg and it was a bullet wasted. He didn't realize he was shooting at a man who counted himself dead, who had nothing to lose by coming on.

Denver reeled onto the porch with guns roaring. And Yuma Miles seemed to jerk, to quiver and fold up as he spun back against the side of the doorway and dropped. Denver stumbled over him into the house kitchen where a glass lamp burned brightly.

"Abby!" he cried thickly. "Where are you, Abby?"

Fists beat on a door in the side wall of the kitchen. A key was in the outside of the lock. A small, shelf-lined storeroom was beyond the door—and in it Abby McKnight, disheveled, pale.

She cried out with pity as she saw Denver's bloody face.

"Anyone else in the house?" Denver gasped.

"There wasn't a few minutes ago."

"Run out the back door. You've got a minute to get away."

"We'll try it."

Denver lurched against the wall. His leg was going numb and useless. "Run on ahead," he told her.

Abby took in his condition with a glance and shook her head. "I won't leave you like this."

Arguing wouldn't move her when she spoke in this fashion. Denver wasted no time trying.

"Help me get the doors fastened," he said. "They'll be here quick."

"The front door is already locked." Abby darted past him, slammed the back door, turned a key that was in the lock, and blew out the lamp.

"I want a gun," she said from the blackness. "I . . . I can shoot."

"Not when you're falling off a wagon," Denver reminded her wryly. "Wait'll I load this one."

He was leaning against the wall. His hands were shaking as he tore cartridges out of the belt loops and thumbed them in.

"They're outside," Abby warned breathlessly.

Denver had heard the voices. "Where's Hayden?"

"He left that man to watch me until they killed Doc Middleton."

"Here's a gun. Doc's cornered across the street."

"I know," Abby said with a breathless calm that showed plainly how she was fighting her emotions. "I signed my lease on the mine over to Hayden when he promised he'd let Doc leave town without harm. And . . . and as soon as he had the signed paper, he laughed at me. He said Doc would go out in a coffin after they were through with him. He . . . he lied to me."

"What did you expect?" Denver said, trying to keep from groaning. "Help me into the front room. They'll be trying to get in."

She put an arm around him. Denver's arm was tightly around her shoulders as he hobbled into the dark front room. He held her tighter than was necessary, and said from a dry throat: "It'd have to happen this way. The only girl I ever saw who meant anything to me."

VIII

Abby's arm held him closely. "Do you mean that?" she said unsteadily.

"You know I do."

"If you'd only said it at the cabin, I'd have gone."

"I guess I didn't know it so well then."

"I did. I wanted you to say it." Abby's voice wavered. "You're bleeding. You're hurt badly. And Hayden will try to kill you."

Denver kissed her hair. They were in the dark front room. The guns throwing lead at Doc Middleton had gone silent. Men were gathering near the white house, shouting, calling to one another.

"We'll find a way out," Denver lied. "I came after gold, but you're worth more than all the gold in these mountains. I won't lose you now."

"Of course, we'll find a way out," Abby said in a choked voice. He could tell she didn't believe it, either.

"Listen," Denver said feverishly, "the gold's not in the San Rico. Just before he was killed, your father had a hunch it wasn't there. Long Tom Forbes brought Jim Short here to test the hunch. Jim drove a new cut that found the high-grade. The ore that Long Tom showed came out of the Silver Girl. Jim wrote me and puttered around waiting for me to come. Look for the gold in the new cut where Jim was working."

Abby was crying softly. "We'll both look there."

"Sure, honey."

But that was wrong, and Abby knew it. Mort Hayden would at least get Denver this night. And then get Doc Middleton and Charley Moose, the Indian. And only Mort Hayden knew what would happen to Abby then. Hayden would still be cock-of-the-walk in San Rico.

That was Mort Hayden's voice now, shouting outside. "Who's in the house there?"

Denver reeled to the door. "Come in and find out, Hayden!"

Two bullets splintered through the door. Hayden's furious voice followed the shots.

"It's young Forbes! Get him out o' there! Burn the house down if you have to!"

"Ain't there a woman in there?" a man asked.

"I don't know! I don't give a damn! Burn Forbes out!"

Abby gasped. "Will he do it?"

"If he can," Denver said quietly. "He's got your mine lease. You don't matter any more. He'll burn us out and their guns'll be waiting." He groaned again. "If you'd only made a run for it. . . ."

Abby's hand groped for his. "I'm glad I'm here."

She meant it, too. Denver held her hand fiercely, and then, as guns opened up outside and bullets slammed through the frame walls and smashed window glass, he ordered: "Get in the kitchen and lie down on the floor. I'll keep them away as much as I can."

"With that leg?" Abby scoffed. "I'll help as much as I can."

She moved from window to window, room to room. Bullets were ripping through doors, walls, shattering windows, raking the dark rooms inside. Denver hobbled from window to window, firing at gun flashes. Abby found guns, belts of ammunition in one of the rooms. They could be prodigal now with bullets.

Denver could hear the crash of her gun in different parts of the house. His nerves stayed tight for the cry that would tell she was struck by a bullet. And there was tragedy in the thought that all this was doing them no good.

He thought with increasing bitterness of the Cross T men. They'd had time to get here. Maybe Old Man Higgins had changed his mind. The Cross T didn't have enough riders, anyway, to clean out this bunch.

Neither he nor Abby saw the man who fired the house. Someone crawled underneath. Denver smelled the acrid smoke, saw the red flicker of fire wavering on the ground outside.

Then, faster than one would have thought possible, the fire caught and spread under the house. Smoke began to billow up past the windows. The first tongues of flame leaped up the sides.

Abby came into the front room and stood beside Denver. Her voice was very quiet. "It won't be long now, will it?"

"There's still a chance for you," Denver said hoarsely. "Walk out there without a gun. They won't shoot you."

"They'll have to shoot me when they shoot you," Abby said in the same quiet voice.

Smoke was seeping through the floors, billowing in the broken windows. Oven-like heat was filling the house. Tongues of flame, snaking up over the front porch, cast a weird dancing glow about them.

"Get back against the wall where they can't see us," Denver ordered harshly, and choked on the smoke.

There was light now to make out her slim presence beside him. To see the heart-breaking pallor and calm of her face. Abby looked up at him and forced a tremulous smile. Denver almost cried out against the bitter hopelessness that seized him. He kissed her fiercely. They clung together for a moment.

The gunmen outside were still shooting in the house at them. But there was no need to watch the doors, the windows. Mort Hayden's men were not trying to get in at them now. They had only to wait around the grisly red halo. Buzzards waiting for the dead.

Abby was coughing, wiping her eyes. Smoke was thick now. The heat had become a terrible living thing that pressed on them, snapped, sucked at resistance. Red, vicious spots began to appear in the floors as the fire ate through. The *snap* and *crackle* of burning wood was drowning out all other sounds. Through the north windows they could see long, leaping tongues of flame, masses of sparks blowing wildly on the hard night wind.

"This'll burn the rest of the town down," Denver choked.

Abby was coughing violently and clinging to his arm. Clinging, Denver realized, as if she had little strength left. He was close to a dazed stupor himself.

With a flash of clarity, Denver realized how terrible the heat had become. Abby couldn't stand much more of it. The floor was quivering. At any moment it might collapse and drop them into that bath of flame below. A sort of madness seized him at the thought. He had to get her out of here, no matter what happened outside.

The gunmen outside had been gripped by the excitement. Denver could hear them yelling wildly. Through the fire's roar he could hear the redoubled sounds of their guns. A red eye appeared in the front door as a fresh bullet hole let in fire glow from outside.

Clumsily Denver made sure his gun and Abby's gun were loaded and took them both. He had to shout to make himself heard.

"We've got to go out! Stay behind me! If I fall, drop down and lie still! Understand?"

Abby nodded.

Gritting his teeth, Denver found strength to help her to the door. A moment he stood there, panting, choking, gathering what little strength he had left. Then he fumbled for the key, yanked the door open, and plodded doggedly through. He couldn't run. Abby couldn't have run, either.

Now they could hear the gunfire and bawling shouts more plainly. Smoke-blinded eyes could barely make out a shadowy figure darting here and there across the street.

The front porch was blazing all around, but they stumbled off it into the blessed coolness of the night wind— stumbled on, with Denver's guns crashing at those indistinct figures out there in the red-lighted night.

He heard a bullet scream close to his head, but couldn't see where it came from as he stumbled and almost fell. Men were shouting ahead of him. Dimly he made out men scattering as if they were afraid of his gunfire.

Now he could see that other buildings to the north of Hayden's house were burning. The San Rico Bar was afire. The red glow of flames seemed to be spreading over the whole town. Fire and death riding like wild horses over Mort Hayden's San Rico.

From streaming eyes, Denver saw in the red light that filled the street a small figure holding a rifle and coming toward them in a crouching run. His gun spurted. He stopped to aim better.

"Doc Middleton!" Abby screamed. She caught Denver's arm.

Denver stood swaying, blinking, trying to see. And the weakness that had been sapping at him like the fire under Hayden's house buckled his knees and dropped him where he stood.

He struggled to his knees, bringing the guns up, and found Abby kneeling beside him, trying to stop him, crying at him: "It's Doc Middleton!"

And then a panting voice, panting and whiskey-husky, burst out accusingly before him: "First time I ever had a patient meet me with two guns going wide open. You're all blood, young fellow. Let's see what's the matter with you before my office burns down an' I can't get at my things."

"You're crazy!" Denver said wildly. "Watch out for Hayden's men!"

"They're busy," Doc Middleton said. "Riders from the Cross T and two other ranches hit town, found everybody watching the fire, an' hit 'em like hell hits the sinful. I saw Mort Hayden killed a few minutes ago. Where you hurt? You look like you're dying."

"Ah, Denver," Abby cried as her arms went around him.

And Doc Middleton's plaintive voice reached Denver a moment later. "No dyin' man ever held a girl like that. When you two get through, come down to my office for patchin' up."

About the Author

T. T. Flynn was born Thomas Theodore Flynn, Jr., in Indianapolis, Indiana. He was the author of over 100 Western stories for such leading pulp magazines as Street & Smith's *Western Story Magazine*, Popular Publications' *Dime Western*, and Dell's *Zane Grey's Western Magazine*. He lived much of his life in New Mexico and spent much of his time on the road, exploring the vast terrain of the American West. His descriptions of the land are always detailed, but he used them not only for local color but also to reflect the heightening of emotional distress among the characters within a story. Following the Second World War, Flynn turned his attention to the book-length Western novel and in this form also produced work that has proven imperishable. Five of these novels first appeared as original paperbacks, most notably *The Man from Laramie* (1954) which was also featured as a serial in *The Saturday Evening Post* and subsequently made into a memorable motion picture directed by Anthony Mann and starring James Stewart, and *Two Faces West* (1954) which deals with the problems of identity and reality and served as the basis for a television series. He was highly innovative and inventive and in later novels, such as *Night of the Comanche Moon* (Five Star Westerns, 1995), concentrated on deeper psychological issues as the source for conflict, rather than more elemental motives like greed. Flynn is at his best in stories that com-

bine mystery—not surprisingly, he also wrote detective fiction — with suspense and action in an artful balance. The
psychological dimensions of Flynn's Western fiction came
increasingly to encompass a confrontation with ethical prin-
ciples about how one must live, the values that one must
hold dear above all else, and his belief that there must be a
balance in all things. The cosmic meaning of the mortality
of all living creatures had become for him a unifying meta-
phor for the fragility and dignity of life itself. *Gunsmoke* will
be his next Five Star Western.